In the

She'd cleaned the blood off her her beautiful alabaster skin. It didn't steal from her essence, though. An essence that drew Iris in and made her curious to know more about the woman.

"Thank you for coming so quickly." It was easy for Iris to hear the fear in her words as she shook Cal's hand. "I don't know what to do next."

"That's why you called us," Cal assured her in his even yet commanding tone, slightly louder than his normal voice. "Dr. Roth, let me introduce you to Iris Knowles, our cybersecurity expert who will work with you to resolve this situation."

Iris stuck her hand out to shake while staring at the doctor's shoes. That made it easier for her to make physical contact with strangers.

Rebecca slid her hand into Iris's, and the sensation was difficult to describe.

Iris knew she was supposed to speak but struggled to form words as Rebecca's touch overwhelmed her.

DEADLY SECURITY BREACH

KATIE METTNER

Harlequin
INTRIGUE

For the real Walter and Zafar.
You got your wish! Thank you for being a friend.

Harlequin INTRIGUE™

MIX Paper | Supporting responsible forestry FSC® C021394 www.fsc.org

Recycling programs for this product may not exist in your area.

ISBN-13: 978-1-335-69040-1

Deadly Security Breach

For questions and comments about the quality of this book, please contact us at CustomerService@Harlequin.com.

Harlequin Enterprises ULC
22 Adelaide St. West, 41st Floor
Toronto, Ontario M5H 4E3, Canada
www.Harlequin.com

HarperCollins Publishers
Macken House, 39/40 Mayor Street Upper,
Dublin 1, D01 C9W8, Ireland
www.HarperCollins.com

Printed in Lithuania

Katie Mettner wears the title of "the only person to lose her leg after falling down the bunny hill" and loves decorating her prosthetic leg to fit the season. She lives in Northern Wisconsin with her own happily-ever-after and spends the day writing romantic stories with her sweet puppy by her side. Katie has an addiction to coffee and dachshunds and a lessening aversion to Pinterest—now that she's quit trying to make the things she pins.

Books by Katie Mettner

Harlequin Intrigue

Secure Watch

Dark Web Investigation
Tracing Her Stolen Identity
Deadly Security Breach

Secure One

Going Rogue in Red Rye County
The Perfect Witness
The Red River Slayer
The Silent Setup
The Masquerading Twin
Holiday Under Wraps

Visit the Author Profile page at Harlequin.com.

CAST OF CHARACTERS

Dr. Rebecca Roth—As the head biology scientist at a remote research facility in North Dakota, Bec works on some of the nastiest viruses in the world. She's never felt unsafe, until she wakes to discover cyber-hackers have commandeered her lab. She doesn't know who wants their deadliest virus, but she knows who to call.

Iris Knowles—Iris has been neurodivergent since suffering a traumatic brain injury as a child. Dealing with extreme anxiety is no picnic, but working for Secure Watch has helped her find stability and safety. All that changes when she's tapped to regain control of a lab filled with pathogens that could take out half the world's population. Unfortunately, she'll have to travel there to do it.

Dr. Walter Hoerman—As the head administrator for the Research Center of The Advancement of Antigenics, he should have done more research before accepting Ignis Cerebri into their lab. Now, it may be too late.

Declan Moss—As one of the newest members of Secure One, this is Declan's chance to prove to Cal that he's more than a pretty face.

Zac Wells—As a Secure One/Secure Watch team member, Zac is versatile in all security aspects, from personal to cyber. His expertise will be needed if his team and the rest of the world want to walk away from this job intact.

Chapter One

The snick of the ventilation system engaging woke Rebecca Roth from a deep sleep. She'd always been a sound sleeper but a light sleeper—meaning she was well rested, even if the slightest sound woke her too early. A glance at the clock told her it was barely 4:00 a.m., but there was no way she was going back to work on that vaccine before 6:00 a.m. and at least two cups of coffee.

She snuggled back into the pillows and tugged the blankets around her neck. Fall had arrived in North Dakota. While it hadn't snowed yet, it was late October, and the temperatures dropped at night to nearly freezing. With her bedroom in a concrete bunker below ground, it made for a cold start to the day. She had started her tenure here in May and wasn't looking forward to the winter temperatures, if the last few weeks were any indication.

When she got her PhD in cell, molecular, health and disease biology, she had no plans to make her home in the middle of nowhere North Dakota. Still, when the opportunity came up to work as the head scientist at the Research Center of The Advancement of Biogenics, she couldn't turn it down. Not when it gave her invaluable experience creating vaccines for new viruses and was the feather in her cap that she'd need to get a faculty position at a university. She planned to work here for a year, make some inroads on vaccines, and then apply for positions nationwide. Once she started publishing papers about her work at the research center, the possibility that someone would come looking for her was very real.

Currently, she worked with a limited number of people due to an incredibly deadly virus residing in her lab. Only the head of the research center, Dr. Walter Hoerman, and their lab tech, Zafar Zimmer, spent time in the center with her. Other than the people who made deliveries of food and supplies, she saw no one else during her days here. It was essential to keep their team small and protect themselves and the rest of the world from the deadly pathogens hidden within their walls. Her mind's eye immediately zipped to Ignis Cerebri, the scientific name for the deadliest virus she'd ever encountered. The brain-burning virus, as she called it, went straight to the brain, where it slowly and painfully burned brain cells until the patient died.

Rebecca had finished the vaccine and was now moving into the testing phase of the process. It was imperative that she finish each step as quickly as possible so it could be tested on live subjects, since each failure would send them back to the starting line. Without a vaccine for this virus, the world would have a pandemic on their hands unlike anything they'd ever seen. A shudder went through her, and she flipped to her back to stare at the grating on the ceiling. At thirty-five, she had enough money and experience to be anywhere but here. She'd left home at sixteen and had only gotten this far in life because of the kindness of strangers, so she wanted her work to matter to those who stepped up to help her when she needed it.

She supposed most people would say they were doing it for their family, but she was dead to them the moment she came out as gay at sixteen when her *Rumspringa* began. Being Amish and gay meant her options were limited in the community: she could remain in the closet, marry and raise kids while hating every second of her life forever, or break out during *Rumspringa* and accept that she could never go back. Neither were easy choices. Not when your formal education ended in the eighth grade. At fourteen, boys were taught vocational skills to learn a trade while the girls continued learning about running the home and farm. What little science she'd learned in school intrigued her and made her want to know more, so when *Rumspringa* hit, she went straight to the public library and read all the books about science and how science impacts the world that she could find. That was the moment she'd made her decision, knowing full well it would be difficult. But she couldn't live a lie forever. That's not living, and she wanted to experience all the wonderful things the world offered, including love.

With a deep and heavy sigh, Rebecca—Bec as her friends called her—tossed back the covers and sat up. She wasn't going back to sleep, so she might as well make that coffee and get started on her workday. Dr. Hoerman had a house outside the research center, so he wouldn't be in until at least nine, and then he'd work until three or four and waltz back out to carry on his life elsewhere. She'd been the head scientist for five months, and it was easy to see why they couldn't retain one for much longer than that. The scientists weren't the problem. Management was the problem. She had contemplated leaving at month four but needed the win of a properly performing vaccine on her résumé. She hoped she'd have that by this time next year, at the latest. The isolation here could get to a person, and she hadn't even experienced a winter in North Dakota. If things kept going as they were, she might have to leave sooner rather than later. Dr. Hoerman was nice but did nothing to help her with the research. It was hard to think about devoting years of your life to a cause no one else seemed interested in.

Even through her thick wool socks, the concrete floor was freezing, so she hurried to the adjoining bathroom to prepare for the day. Her biggest fear, and the only reason she stayed, was that if she left, no one would finish the vaccine, and the world would suffer because she couldn't hack it. Guilt had no place in the life of a scientist, but this virus was unlike anything she'd ever seen, so for the good of humanity, she had to stay. A hot shower, hotter coffee and warm oatmeal was her plan, and then she'd get down to the business of the day—saving the world.

"JUST CHECKING IN, BEC," Dr. Hoerman said when he entered the office and research space.

Rebecca gasped and turned to the doctor, dressed in khakis and a flannel shirt. There was no sense in dressing up when no one saw you anyway. They only wore business attire when they had conference calls with other labs. Today was not one of those days.

"Walter, you scared me," she said, her hand to her chest.

"I'm early," he said with a wink. He reminded her more of a lumberjack than a doctor but had been a brilliant mind in science for years before becoming the admin of this research center. "Couldn't sleep, so thought I'd get some work done."

It was nearly 7:00 a.m., and she was just getting started with work. Her earlier resolve to get up and work had been curbed by the hot shower that had relaxed her, and she'd fallen asleep for a few hours. She'd needed the extra rest, but now she felt great and hoped today would be the day she could concentrate on the next steps to bring the vaccine to the testing phase.

"I couldn't sleep, either," she said, lowering herself to her chair. "It must be in the water."

Walter snorted. "More like the attitude of a teenager. My sister called and wanted me to talk to my nephew."

"That doesn't sound fun," Bec agreed. "But family is everything, so you have to be there for them." She said it as though she had any. That was the most challenging part of her decision to part ways with her community. Knowing she now had nieces and nephews that she would never meet and siblings she would never see again. Looking back over the last nineteen years of her life, she knew she'd made the right decision by leaving, though. There was no way she would have survived in that community living the life she was expected to live when it would all be a lie.

"You say that like you understand family on a different level," Walter said, sitting at his desk.

"It's an easy lesson to learn when you live more of your life without family than with it. That's the breaks, though. All I can do is hope they're doing well. I know that the people I've met along the way, those who helped me succeed when they didn't have to, are my family now."

Walter nodded as he turned on his computer, so with a sigh, Bec did the same. It was a melancholy morning. Thinking or talking about her family always made her feel that way. What she said was the truth. She'd been gone from the Amish community for longer than she'd been in it, and those people were a memory now. She did hope they were all well, but she also understood she was only alive and well because she left them to be herself.

"Are you seeing this?" Walter asked, and his tone of voice told her there was a problem as her computer flickered to life.

All her attention was on the screen now, and she froze with her hands over the keyboard. The screen was black with a white ace of spades filling it. Quickly, she gave the computer several commands, and when that didn't work, she tried to pull up recovery mode.

"Should I restart it?" Walter asked from his desk.

"No!" Bec exclaimed, her heart hammering in her chest as she turned to him. "I think we've been hit with malware. If you restart your computer, it could brick all the devices."

"Brick them?" he asked, his head tipped in confusion.

"Render them useless. If we lose control of the systems that the main computers run, and somehow the containment system goes down, everyone is dead."

Walter froze as the implications of this hit him. "This is bad."

"This is catastrophic," Bec whispered, her gaze drawn back to the computer where a message appeared as though someone was typing it one letter at a time.

Stay tuned... More to come! 4C3

"Who is 4C3?" Walter asked, his voice relaying the same shock and fear coursing through her.

"A phantom, and if we aren't careful, that's what we'll be."

"Can you fix this?" Walter asked, coming around his desk to face her.

"No, but I know who can. They won't be cheap."

"The time for sparing expense is over," Walter said, squeezing her shoulder. "We have to protect the lab's assets to protect the country. Call them."

Rebecca grabbed her phone and clicked the home button, half expecting that to be bricked. When it wasn't, she let out a breath and opened a browser tab. There was only one team that she could think of who could get them out of this jam. She just had to pray she could help them understand the magnitude of the problem and get them here quickly.

Chapter Two

Iris patted around on the bedside table for her glasses until her fingers wrapped around the frames. Once she slid them onto her face, everything came into focus again. Her double vision prevented her from doing anything without them, but it disappeared once she had the prism lenses on. Just another little gift the traumatic brain injury had given her. That happened when she was seven, so after twenty-six years, she was used to everything required to keep herself going in a world that didn't understand her.

Something had woken her, but she had sworn she'd shut her phone off before bed. The clock by her bed said it was barely 7:30 a.m., which meant she'd only been asleep for three hours. She'd been working on tracking down someone from a client's past last night and hadn't wanted to stop and break her momentum. By the time 3:00 a.m. rolled around, she'd found the guy responsible for stalking their client, and the last she'd heard, he was being arrested. If there was one thing she loved about her job, it was keeping people safe. She wished that she'd had someone doing that for her all those years ago. That was probably why she found so much joy in her work here at Secure Inc. The company encompassed her employer Secure Watch, along with the personal security company called Secure One. She could use her computer skills to protect people in a way her friends at Secure One couldn't—even with their fancy guns and bodyguards.

There was satisfaction in knowing the messed-up pathways in her brain that resulted from her injury had helped her as much as they'd hurt her. Her mother used to say everything in life was a trade-off, and she wasn't wrong. It was a struggle to remember that when dealing with the result of her injuries, but getting wins like she did last night helped keep her going.

Iris grabbed her phone and swiped it open, surprised to see an all-call alert from her boss. Something big must have happened in the past three hours because Mina, her boss at Secure Watch, didn't use that alert unless it was an emergency. Since moving to Secure Inc., Iris had finally found the place that played to her strengths and understood her weaknesses. Speaking of weakness, she grabbed her foot drop braces and strapped them on before slipping into her shoes. That was yet another gift from her TBI. Some people could walk short distances without braces, but she hadn't won that lottery, either. When she walked without her braces, her toes dragged along the floor, often tripping her up until she face-planted. She didn't have time to worry about that today since Mina had only given her ten minutes to meet everyone in the conference room. She didn't have much time to prepare.

After quickly using the facilities and taking time to run a brush through her hair and across her teeth, she grabbed a clean shirt and a pair of pants. The idea of everyone gathering in one room always made Iris nervous. She didn't do well in large groups due to her anxiety. Not to mention, she struggled to follow conversations that involved a lot of voices all at once. Her brain couldn't sort it all out, making her even more anxious. Maybe she should text Mina and tell her she was sick. After grabbing her phone from the side of the bed, she opened the app, but her fingers were shaking too much to type.

There was a rap on her door, and she jumped, a short scream leaving her lips. "It's me, Iris. You're okay," Mina called through the door.

Iris rushed to the door and threw it open to see her boss standing there with Hannah Grace, her three-year-old daughter. "Iris!" Hannah squealed and threw herself around her legs in a hug.

Iris dropped to one knee and gave the little girl a proper hug. From the moment she'd met Hannah, they'd been best buds. She found so much joy in watching the little girl learn and grow each day, and it reminded her that childhood can be innocent and joyful instead of traumatic and scary. "Hi, sweetheart. You're up early."

"Mommy and Daddy have to work, and Aunt Sadie is making breakfast, so I had to stay with Mommy. I'll be really quiet in the meeting."

"You're always a good girl, Hannah," Mina assured her daughter, ruffling her hair. "The meeting won't take long, and then you can have your French toast. I need to talk to Iris for a minute, okay?"

"Okay, Mommy," Hannah said, running to the corner where Iris kept a doll and a few other toys for her to play with.

"I was just texting you," Iris said, not making eye contact with her boss. After the accident, she struggled with many things, including social skills that most people could do without thinking.

"I figured," Mina agreed. "I know all calls make you nervous, but there's nothing to worry about. It's just you, me and some of the guys from Secure One. We have an imminent situation, and we need your help."

"You would probably be better at whatever it is. You're one of the best hackers the FBI ever had," Iris said, staring at the floor.

Mina tipped her chin up, so Iris had to make eye contact. She didn't like it, but she did it because Mina was her friend. "Iris, we need you. It's not about hacking. It's about securing assets. We need your expertise. You're the only one we trust to get the job done. Are you in?"

"You can do it, Iris!" Hannah said, walking over from where she'd been playing. "You're the best at catching the bad guys, just like Daddy!"

Iris couldn't help but laugh as she glanced down at the blond-haired beauty. "Thank you, sweetheart, but your daddy is much braver than I am."

"Everyone in this building would disagree with that, Iris," Mina said. "Bravery comes in many different forms and definitions. You are one of the bravest people I know, so harness that because we need you. Okay?"

Iris forced herself to hold her boss's gaze. She'd been practicing with Hannah since kids made that easier, and now she could do it with adults for longer, too. She nodded. "I'm ready."

Iris took Hannah's hand, and they walked to the conference room together, where Cal and two of his men, Zac Wells and Declan Moss, were waiting for them.

"Hi," Iris said, staring at the floor. "Are we late? I didn't mean to make anyone late."

"Good morning, Iris. Remember, you're fine being yourself here," Cal said, which he said a lot when she was in the room.

She nodded and slid into a seat next to Mina, allowing Hannah to hop up on her lap to color on a pad at the table while the team talked. The sweet little girl had been born in the med bay and raised in the building all her life, so to her, this was a regular Tuesday morning. To Iris, it was anything but that. Her belly was full of butterflies, and her anxiety was rocketing as Cal worked the remote to get something up on the large screen in the room.

"We got a call this morning from the Research Center for Advanced Biogenics," Mina said to begin. "From what I understand, the research center is privately owned by a group of investors but run by a scientist who obtains quotes and jobs for different types of research from other labs, government agencies and universities. There's also a lead scientist who works on those projects. Their system has been compromised due to malware, and they need help restoring their programs. We have a recording of a call I had with Dr. Rebecca Roth, the lead scientist at the center, about the situation. We'll play that for you and then make our game plan."

Cal clicked the remote, and a woman wearing a white lab coat filled the screen. Iris quickly took in the space around her and noted the laboratory rooms, high stainless-steel tables, and several rooms separated by sliding glass doors. A man sat behind her in a flannel shirt and jeans. He was older, easily in his sixties, and nervous, if the way he tapped his thigh with his fingers was any indication.

Whoever he was, he was letting Dr. Roth do the talking. When Iris focused on Dr. Roth, her heart paused in her chest and then resumed in a rhythm that was as atypical as her brain. For the first time in too long, it felt…normal. Slow. Unhurried. Confident. Peaceful. Iris hadn't felt that way since she was seven years old.

"This morning, the lab computers were attacked," Rebecca explained. She was beautiful, with long wavy brown hair and the most bottomless brown eyes Iris had ever seen. They were filled with a pain she knew all too well, and maybe that's why she was instantly drawn to her. It was the pain of knowing you didn't belong anywhere or to anyone. "The system is locked, and this message is on all the computers." Rebecca turned the camera to show a screen that revealed an ace of spades and the message, *Stay tuned... More to come! 4C3*

Cal paused the video and turned to the assembled group. "Here comes the part about why it's imperative we do this job quickly and efficiently." He clicked Play on the remote again.

"Our facility currently harbors the deadliest virus on the planet. Ignis Cerebri, sometimes called the brain-burning virus, will make COVID-19 look like the common cold, and we all know how brutal that virus was. Unfortunately, with Ignis Cerebri, the victims wouldn't know they came into contact with it until they died, and by then, they could have spread it to many more people. There's no way to slow the progression of the disease or treat it that we know of yet, so my job was to develop a vaccine, which I recently completed. I was ready to move into the testing phase and start writing and publishing documentation of the process. What that means is, I don't know if the vaccine works on humans, nor is there enough for a widespread outbreak of this disease. If the containment room security is compromised and the virus escapes through the center's air exchange, there's no way to predict what will happen. Worse yet, if Ignis Cerebri were to fall into the wrong hands, it could be a biological weapon of Armageddon proportions."

Transfixed by the woman on the screen, Iris knew she had to help her. She'd utilize every tool in the command center and work every second of the day to fix this without even meeting her. Rebecca Roth was captivating from a distance, and she appreciated how in control she was during the report. She had a scientific mind, which Iris could appreciate beyond anything else. It wasn't until Cal cleared his throat that she realized he'd paused the video. Turning slowly with her cheeks heating, she waited for him to continue.

"We need all hands on deck with this one. Dr. Roth says they're locked out of the labs since they don't have access to the program that runs them. That means she doesn't know if the containment system still holds the viruses."

"Does this 4C3 guy have access?" Zac asked. Although he was a relatively new hire to Secure One, he had a mile-long résumé protecting people.

"Ace," Iris mumbled. "4C3 is his call sign online, but you call him Ace when it's converted."

"That's all Greek to me," Zac said, shaking his head. "I'm not up on all the lingo."

Declan and Zac sometimes did double duty for Secure Inc. They worked as security guards on large jobs but could also install security systems, which gave them rudimentary computer skills, at least in comparison to her own. Iris liked and respected them as the kind of guys who could do everything and make it look easy.

"The lingo," Cal said with haste, "will only get worse in this case before it gets better. I don't understand much of what Dr. Roth told me other than 'the deadliest virus' and 'it can't fall into the wrong hands' part. Do we all agree on that?" Everyone's heads nodded.

Mina took over from there. "Good, then the plan is as follows. The research center is in the middle of nowhere North Dakota, to protect the general public, but that makes it difficult to get there quickly. Cal will fly the three of you to the research center to shave hours off your travel time."

"Wait," Iris said, "that would include me, right?" Mina nodded with a brow up, and just as quickly, Iris was shaking her head no. "That's not—no. I can't do that. You know how I work, Mina!" That peaceful rhythm she had enjoyed for a few moments was gone, replaced by the banging of her heart against her ribs as she tried not to hyperventilate. The very idea of leaving Secure Inc. and traveling to someplace unknown would send her into a panic attack if she thought too hard about it, so she wouldn't. She wouldn't think about it. Couldn't.

Deep breath, Iris. That inner voice reminded her she was still safe at Secure Inc.

"You think you can't do it," Cal said before Mina could speak. "But I disagree. You can do anything you put your mind to, which you've proven repeatedly."

Mina turned to her and leaned in on the table. "We all know you need things done a certain way, but not only does Dr. Roth need you, but the country needs you.

Maybe even the world. There's no question in my mind that you can do this."

"But you could do it," Iris repeated, just in case Mina had changed her mind. "You could go, and I could run interference here for you."

"While that sounds like a good solution, it's not," Mina said gently. "We're in the middle of some other cases here, and I'm also needed for those. You are the only person who can put their entire focus into helping the research center gain control of its system and, therefore, the viruses. You're the person for this job."

"We got you, Iris," Zac said, turning to her but avoiding direct eye contact as he knew that was the best way to make her comfortable. "We'll run security outside the center while you work through the program to get the system back online. Declan will be there if you need an extra hand with a computer issue, but for the most part, our job is to support you by keeping the center safe."

"He's right," Cal said, his voice firm. "Once you get there, you'll be working in an environment not that much different from here. The only people you'll deal with will be Dr. Roth and Dr. Hoerman, but that will be on your terms as you need information or help regarding how the system works. We need you, Iris."

"Will I lose my job if I say no?" She glanced at the two people in the room who controlled her fate in an attempt to read their expressions, but they were stoic.

"Absolutely not," Mina said. "We'll just have to make a different plan."

She might not lose her job, but Iris could tell they'd be disappointed with her if she disagreed. The deep brown eyes of Rebecca Roth floated through her mind again, and a shiver racked her. Dr. Roth needed help, and for a reason that Iris couldn't explain, she wanted to be the one to offer it.

"Time is of the essence, and I'm fast at what I do. I don't like to travel, but I'll do it for you and Cal," she finally said, stroking Hannah's long blond hair. Maybe she was also intrigued enough by Rebecca to want to meet her. "I'll have to take an extra dose of my medication, though, so I'll be dependent on you."

Cal gave her a finger gun with his prosthetic hand. "You think you're not a team player, but you always come through for us. Just remember that we've got you, and we all know how to protect and keep you safe. I know you're worried, scared and nervous, but you have nothing to fear. We got you."

It was always easy for someone else to say that, but it was more complicated when she lived with a brain that had pathways that didn't link up the same way neurotypical brains did. Her therapist always told her that was okay because the world needed people whose pathways were different, or we'd never solve a problem. She was right in theory, but those misplaced pathways made her life more difficult in practice. Still, she trusted Cal and Mina. They wouldn't ask her to do a job they wouldn't do themselves if they had the skills. Did Mina have the skills? Yes, but she was right—she'd be pulled in too many directions to do the job quickly and efficiently. On the other hand, Iris was skilled at shutting out everything but the keys under her fingers and the code flying across the screen. Despite the welling panic in her chest, she was the best person for the job.

Mina's computer started ringing out of the blue, and

when she answered it, Dr. Roth's face filled the screen. Iris noticed how terrified her eyes were right before she noticed the streaks of blood on her face and the cuts on her cheeks. "Dr. Hoerman was just kidnapped! I need help!"

Chapter Three

Bec paced the lab, wishing they had more space for her to stretch her anxious legs. Normally, she'd go outside for a walk, but she didn't want to leave the building in case something else happened or another message came in from this 4C3 guy. Unable to access his computer, Dr. Hoerman sat in his office, tapping his fingers. She had suggested he call the investors of the facility, but he wasn't ready to do that yet. He had said that until they had more information about what 4C3 wanted, there was little he could tell them. She figured he was hedging his bets, hoping that this was a little hiccup rather than something more extensive. Her gut feeling was that he would be disappointed. For some reason, they'd been targeted, and now it was up to them to save the world from these highly deadly diseases.

"I thought this couldn't happen to the computers at the center," she said on a trip past Walter's office.

He leaned forward and clasped his hands together on his desk. "That's what I was told," he agreed.

"By the board?"

"And the team that wrote the programs for the center. They said no hacker could take it over."

"How long ago did they say that?" she asked as she paused by his door.

"Why would that matter?"

"Because when it comes to computers, one you buy today is outdated before you take it out of the package. There has to be an IT team keeping the system running smoothly, right?"

"You're asking the wrong guy," he said, giving her the palms up gesture. "I would have to assume the investors employ someone who keeps things running. We've never had a problem before."

"Before today," Bec added, starting her pacing again. "All we can do is hope Secure Watch can fix this disaster before we have a bigger problem. I still think you should notify the board, Walter. We don't want to blindside them if a ransom comes in."

"A ransom?"

"What do you think that is?" she asked, motioning at the message on her computer. "That's ransomware. At some point, 4C3 will request money in exchange for unlocking our systems."

Walter shook his head with an exasperated huff. "I don't understand a thing about this stuff, Bec."

She walked into his office and leaned on the edge of his desk. "Understand this, Walter. If we don't pay a requested ransom, we will never be able to use these computers again and will have no way to access or control what's behind those doors!" Her arm flung out to point at the labs behind her.

He held up his hands as though to ask for calm. "Okay, as soon as nine o'clock rolls around, I'll reach out to them. I don't have home numbers, only the office number."

"I can accept that," she said, leaving his office to return to her computer. The message on the screen hadn't changed.

Secure Watch was on the way, but they'd be a few hours yet, and Bec was on edge since she hadn't heard anything more from the faceless person who had taken their data hostage. Walter didn't seem to understand the gravity of the situation, but that didn't surprise her. His computer skills were second to none with the programs necessary to run the lab, but computer science wasn't his forte. He was never on the ground floor of computer science as it developed, which is why they'd hired someone to protect their system from hackers. Fat lot of good that did. Her opinion was that no amount of money was too much if it meant keeping the viruses inside their lab from reaching the general public.

What scared Bec the most was that she'd been working at the research center for months and had been led to believe that their cybersecurity was second to none. She was told a cyberattack could never happen to them due to the highly contagious viruses housed in the facility. She was angry that the man who was supposed to be in charge of the center didn't know a hill of beans about it. If she survived this, she'd be rethinking her employment here. Part of her worried she'd accepted this job with her ego instead of considering it from all angles. It may have been about proving that her *lifestyle* didn't mean she couldn't make massive contributions to the world. She may have left the Amish community two decades ago, but there was that little girl inside her who still felt like she had to prove she was worthy of being loved and respected even though she was gay. Those were the words her parents had used. They said she could remain in the community even though she was gay as long as she didn't tell anyone else.

She blew out a breath and forced her mind back into the game. Before she took the job here, it was confirmed that few people knew this building in the middle of the North Dakota plains was anything more than a facility for common scientific research, but now she couldn't be sure. The fact that this hacker had hit them with a computer virus told her they knew where to look.

A door slammed, and she spun around on her heel, only to be thrown backward into the glass from the force of something so deafening the world went silent other than a ringing in her ears. All she could see were bits and pieces of the room around her, and she realized the bright light had partially blinded her.

A man. A mask. A gun.

Barely able to see through the lacelike haze across her vision, she watched the man put the gun to Walter's head. He hooked his arm around her boss's neck and hauled him from the chair, leading him backward through the office and down the hallway. She tried to stand, but the glass behind her shattered and she hit the ground, sure a bullet had slammed into the glass. Her neck was wet, and she swiped at it, stumbling to her feet when she saw the blood covering her palm. She tried to run but felt like she was moving through quicksand, bumping and falling into tables and chairs as she tried to make it down the hallway to save her boss. Her head hurt, and her arm burned, but she had to get to Walter. When she reached the hallway, no one was in sight, which told her it was too late. All she could do was lock down the facility and pray.

THE CHOPPER'S SKIDS touched the ground, and Iris's anxiety ratcheted down one notch as they arrived safely. She'd taken a dose of diazepam before they left since there was no other way she'd ever get into the death trap despite knowing she had to get to the research center. She had to help Dr. Roth get control of their systems before things got worse than they already were. That didn't mean she wanted to make the trip to do it. The fear of unknown places was just one of the things she dealt with after her traumatic brain injury. Traveling didn't bother her as long as she knew what she'd be facing and was traveling in a way that didn't terrify her. Neither was the case today. When she got the job at Secure Watch, she'd been surprisingly excited to move to the property. Within a few weeks, she knew why. The energy there was accepting. No one was better than anyone else, and they understood that everyone had different physical and mental idiosyncrasies that they needed to play to for the team to work cohesively. Somehow, Cal and Mina made everyone feel they were imperative to the team, and today's events showed her why. Sometimes, lives were on the line in this business, and specific team members needed to step up. Today, she was that team member, and because they'd fostered a give-and-take relationship with her over the years, she could trust them and do just that.

After releasing a pent-up breath, Iris grabbed her bag and tossed it over her shoulder, knowing Zac, Declan and Cal would unload her equipment and bring it to the center. Once everything was unloaded and jobs were defined, Cal would head back and leave them to do their work while Mina offered support from Secure Inc. Despite trusting their skills, Iris could tell Cal was nervous about leaving them. Who wouldn't be? In this situation, he was dropping off team members he may never see again if something terrible happened. All the more reason for him not to stay. The fewer people here for her to stress about the better when trying to fix this situation. Besides, she worked better and faster when she was alone. Considering what happened to the other doctor here, time was definitely of the essence.

She tumbled out of the old behemoth of a helicopter and glanced around. There was nothing but pastureland as far as the eye could see, and a mountain range was visible in the distance. The summer wheat blew as a light breeze swept across the stalks, and the rustling of the grain was a reminder that life went on around them, even if they were faced with their own little hell. Something told her Dr. Roth felt that way after what she'd been through this morning, and Iris just wanted to get to the center and help her. She walked around the back of the chopper where Zac and Declan were loading bins and equipment into a UTV. She knew for a fact some of those bins held hazmat suits, but she also knew those wouldn't be enough to protect them from what they'd be dealing with if something from inside their home away from home managed to escape.

Cal spoke to three men in a smaller UTV before he waved as they headed across the field toward the mountains.

"Where did you get these?" Iris asked, staring at the ground. "Who were those guys?"

"A couple of army friends of mine," Cal answered as he approached her. "They loaned us the UTVs for the duration of the stay."

"I don't think we're in the right place. There's nothing here, Cal."

His laughter was gentle when he patted her back. "We're about five miles away from the facility, Iris. We couldn't land close to it and draw attention there. It's better to take the UTVs in. They're so common around here it won't seem out of place."

"Did Dr. Roth call the police?" she asked as he motioned for her to climb into the back seat of a UTV. The vehicle was as big as a Jeep, but it was open to the elements, so she kept her head tucked down out of nervousness as Zac fired it up.

"I'll explain when we're there!" Cal said over the roar of the motor.

Head down and eyes squeezed shut, Iris did her box breathing to keep her anxiety level in check as they bounced and rattled through the wheat to a road. The ride smoothed out considerably then, but she didn't look up. Cal had his hand on her back, which made her feel infinitesimally better about the situation. On the inhale, she pictured Rebecca's face covered in blood, and while she held her breath for four counts, she remembered the fear in her voice as she described what had happened. When she exhaled, she pictured herself at the keyboard, bringing the safety protocols back online to protect everyone from an unseen evil. The imagery allowed her to square her shoulders and lift her head slightly just as Zac slowed the vehicle.

Across the road, a building was half buried inside an earth dome. "You'd never know the terrors of the world are held inside there," she said, noting that Cal nodded from the corner of her eye.

"Which is the point, but obviously, someone knew it was here. And that someone has plans we need to put a stop to. Are you ready?"

"Not even a little bit, but I know I'm part of the solution, so let's do this."

"That's my girl. I'm proud of you every day, but today even more so," he said as Zac rolled the UTV around to the side, where there was a small loading dock. Zac jumped out to start unloading while he waited for Declan to catch up in the other UTV. Cal punched a button by a side door and spoke into the speaker, announcing their arrival to the only person inside—Rebecca Roth.

The door clicked open, and Cal motioned her forward, leaving the guys to deal with the supplies. They walked into a cavernous space that defied the outside dimensions.

"Where are we? I thought this was a lab," she said, and Cal nodded.

"We're in the loading bay. The lab is upstairs."

He pointed at a door marked Stairs, held it open for her and joined her as they went up a flight of stairs that opened into a hallway. Cal turned left, and she followed, noting an employee break room on the right, along with several restrooms.

When they left the hallway, on their right were glass partitions separating multiple labs with sliding doors that opened into the large center workspace. Inside each lab was equipment Iris had no idea how to use, as well as rows of test tubes and hanging ventilation fans.

In the center of the room were large tables for standing while working. That was where a disheveled and nervous woman stood wringing her hands. She'd cleaned the blood off her face, but the cuts were copious and dotted her beautiful alabaster skin. It didn't steal from her essence, though. An essence that drew Iris in and made her curious to know more about the woman. "Thank you for coming so quickly." It was easy to hear the fear in her words as she shook Cal's hand. "I don't know what to do next. My ears are still ringing, so you'll have to speak up."

"That's why you called us," Cal assured her in his even yet commanding tone, slightly louder than his normal voice. "Dr. Roth, let me introduce you to Iris Knowles, our cybersecurity expert, who will work with you to resolve this situation."

Iris stuck her hand out to shake while staring at the doctor's shoes. That made it easier for her to make physical contact with strangers. Rebecca slid her hand into Iris's, and the sensation was difficult to describe. Iris knew she was supposed to speak but struggled to form words as Rebecca's touch overwhelmed her. When her warm palm caressed her skin, all she could think of was sunshine on a rainy day. Iris knew she was here to do a job, so as the doctor released her hand, she lifted her head and made eye contact with the woman for an instant. Rebecca imprinted on her soul in that short moment, sending an unexpected shockwave through her.

"Nice to meet you, Iris," Rebecca said, her voice softer, calmer. "I can't thank you enough for coming."

"It was a lot of work to get here, and I didn't want to come, but I did." Iris grimaced as she stared at the floor. "I'm sorry for saying that."

"Iris has lingering effects from a traumatic brain injury," Cal explained. "She finds traveling to new places overwhelming. She'll need a few minutes to adjust."

"He's right, but I promise it won't interfere with solving your problem. Fair warning that I don't know how to lie or be anything but honest and straightforward, or what some might consider blunt. It's an unfortunate result of having my brain scrambled."

"I understand," Rebecca said, but not in the kind of pitiful voice Iris was used to. Those two words were said with respect, which she proved with her following sentence. "If I can do anything to make it easier for you, don't hesitate to tell me what you need, and I'll make it happen. I prefer honesty over lies anyway, even if the delivery is blunt. We must contain this situation, which will require us to work together as a team."

"Social skills have been difficult for me to learn, and I've tried, but unfortunately, my brain often forgets how to do that, so honest and straightforward is what you'll get from me. Sometimes to a fault, as Cal says," Iris admitted.

"But she always means well," Cal added with a wink.

Rebecca laughed, lifting the mood and Iris's head. "In this situation, be honest to a fault. We're going to need it to get through this."

Iris noted the woman's full lips pull into a thin line as she glanced around the room at the labs. "That is also my assessment," she agreed. "Don't worry, though, Dr. Roth, I won't sleep until you have control of your lab again. My brain is already messed up, so the last thing I want is to feel it burning."

Cal and Rebecca snickered in response to her sentence, which lifted Iris's lips into a smile for the first time since the call sounded this morning. She'd made a joke, and people laughed. A new skill unlocked!

"Please, call me Bec," she said as she motioned them toward a desk where a computer sat. "All my friends do."

"But I'm not your friend," Iris said before she could stop herself. Cal gently grasped her forearm to remind her to be calm.

"Yet," Bec said with a wink. "I have a feeling that will have changed by the time we finish this project. As you can see, all the computers have the same screen and message. It's been hours since we found the message, but nothing has changed, and there have been no ransom requests."

"Unless kidnapping the other doctor was the message," Cal said, motioning at her face.

Iris followed as they walked toward an office strewn with papers and shards of glass. The scene was terrifying, and she hadn't lived through it with a flash-bang and kidnapper. Her heart went out to the woman whose hands shook as she described what happened to her colleague. Iris could only think of one thing to do. She walked over and put her hand on Bec's shoulder. Without pausing her story, Bec laid her hand on hers, and she noticed the scientist's hands stopped shaking immediately.

It was then that Iris realized she could help this woman in more ways than one.

Chapter Four

Rebecca stood around one of the tables in the center workspace with Cal, Iris, Declan and Zac. They were going over the kidnapping step-by-step and making a plan for how to proceed.

"You don't think I should call the police?" Bec asked again. "Won't they hold me responsible for not reporting a crime?"

"They might," Cal said with a nod. "But you can make a case that the message on the computer said more was to come, so you waited to hear from them. We don't know who took Dr. Hoerman. If the people responsible for his kidnapping are watching the property and suddenly it's swarmed by police, they may very well kill him. We should wait for their communication before bringing the authorities in on this, but you'll have to make the final call."

"Like a ransom?" she asked, eyeing everyone around the table. "That would make the most sense, right?"

"I've been doing this job for many years, and it's what my gut tells me," Cal agreed. "I expect it to come in twelve hours or less. They kidnapped him for a reason, and there are only two that I can think of. Money or power. Whoever took him thinks he has control or information about the lab that they can use to their benefit."

"He does," Bec agreed. "He's the one who worked to procure the Ignis Cerebri at this lab."

"So, this is a government facility?" Declan asked, but Bec shook her head.

"No, we're a privately funded research facility with clients from private and public companies and organizations. My job as head scientist is to do whatever is asked scientifically of the client, while it's Walter's job to do all the administrative tasks."

"Do you know who requested that you create a vaccine?" Cal asked, and again, Bec shook her head no.

"That's not my wheelhouse—it was need-to-know information that I didn't need to know."

"Didn't need to know *then*," Zac said. "Now that you do, it's too late."

Bec bit her lip with a nod. "I agree, but he couldn't have told me even if I'd demanded it. I could find out if I logged into his computer, but I can't. Since he had his phone in his hand when he was kidnapped, I can't even look at that."

"Which means Walter is worth ransoming," Zac said.

"Honestly, I'm worth more to them than Walter," she said, rubbing the back of her neck. It was sore from falling earlier when the flash-bang threw her backward. When she dropped her hand, Iris's replaced it. That surprised her but she tried not to let it show. Iris massaged her neck gently, and the warmth of her hand helped Bec focus better on the conversation.

"Because you made the vaccine?" Cal asked, and she nodded.

"Maybe they didn't know that, or it was more of an opportunist kidnapping?" Iris asked.

"Whoever they could take would be better than no one at all?" Cal mused, and heads bobbed around the table.

"The funny part is, they wouldn't have to kidnap any of us if they knew what was inside those labs," Bec said, motioning to her left. "Taking control of the system was enough. We'd have paid anything to get control of it again."

"Let's hope Walter doesn't tell them that," Cal said dryly.

"He won't," Bec assured them. "The only thing he'll do is clam up and say nothing because he works with too many agencies to do anything else."

"The kidnappers will be in touch then," Declan said. "They'll want money in exchange for his life. What we have to decide is if they're working with Ace or if we have two different ransom situations. What other reason would they do this?"

"As long as that ransom isn't the virus," Iris said as she met Bec's gaze. "If it's what you say it is, that's a weapon of mass destruction someone might want to auction off to the highest bidder."

Bec's laughter surprised the other four. "I was hoping none of you would consider that. I should have known that was a pipe dream."

"After the Spiderweb case we worked on a few years ago, nothing would surprise me," Iris said with a shrug.

Bec remembered the case and shuddered. Someone on the dark web had written a program to look like a video game that was anything but that. Had it gone mainstream, the "game" would slowly give the coder the data from every public camera in the free world by planting malware in their operating system. It was a terrorist's dream, and the coder knew that. Unfortunately, the government hadn't yet caught Savant. Fortunately, the woman who discovered the program, Kenley Mason, now a Secure Watch operative, had helped the government write a malware patch to prevent Spiderweb from getting the data from the cameras.

"The Spiderweb case taught us people are always after money, power or both. In this case, I could see them wanting the virus they could sell as a weapon of mass destruction. Unless Walter can convince them that you already have a working vaccine. If he can do that, then they may demand money instead. Declan is correct that we could also be dealing with two different groups looking to get money out of the center, though the odds are high that it would happen all on the same day if they weren't working together. That said, all we can do is wait and see. In the meantime, Iris can work on getting the ventilation system back online," Cal said.

"What about Walter's sister? Should we notify her about the situation?" Bec asked.

"He has a sister?"

"Yes, and at least one nephew, but I don't know her name or where she lives," Bec explained.

"Are they close?" Cal asked.

"I know he talks to his nephew on the phone whenever his sister calls for backup. He doesn't talk much about his family, so I can't say more than that."

"I'll have Mina look into it. I want to keep his family out of it until we get a ransom request, if possible."

"And if Ace does reach out with a ransom request?

Then what do I do?" Bec asked, holding Cal's gaze. She had no idea how to navigate her world now but hated depending on someone else to answer her questions.

"Iris will call Secure Watch immediately, and we can make a plan from there. Trying to do that now is a lesson in futility. Instead of wasting time, we'll be proactive by securing the building while you work on getting the most important aspects of the lab back online. Declan and Zac will patrol the building. If you need anything, radio them using this," he said, holding up a black walkie-talkie. "Unless there's a fire, do not try to leave the building without notifying them. We don't need any unintended casualties."

"We'll be too busy to leave the lab," Iris said, eyeing her equipment. Bec could tell she was aching to set it up. "Give it to me straight, Cal." She turned to her boss. "Are we safe here?"

"As safe as any of us can be right now, Iris," he assured her, his hand on her shoulder. "Declan and Zac have your back with security, and we know you'll get all the important aspects of the lab up and running again quickly."

"I'm glad you have confidence in me."

"We do, or you wouldn't be here," he said, his brow raised. "I also know you'll stop at nothing to protect the entire nation from this virus. Your job is to help Bec do just that and keep Mina updated on each step as you go. If you need help, she's available anytime, so don't hesitate to call her."

"Are you really returning to Secure Inc.?" Declan asked.

"Yes, but not for long," Cal said. "I'll load up equipment and a few more guys, then return to Sinlis Park, the town closest to here. I'll set up a temporary home base there until we have a ransom or a resolution. You two will need to sleep," he said, motioning at Declan and Zac, "but I also want two people patrolling the building at all times. At night, there will be three. We'll run eighteen on and six off, so make good use of those six off. Understood?" Both men nodded, so Cal continued. "I'd like more men to cover the property, but I can't bring an army until we know what the kidnappers want."

"If the kidnappers are watching, won't they notice the security guys anyway?" Bec asked, leaning on the table. Her head hurt, and while she could hear better now, the ringing in her ears made it hard for her to concentrate on the situation.

"There's no way around that," Cal said with a shrug. "I'm shocked you didn't always have security on the building."

"We did," she said, "just not in human form. The biometrics we use to run this lab is our security. There's no way in or out of the building without me or Dr. Hoerman."

"Wait, you mean none at all?" Declan asked, glancing at his boss.

"None," she said again. "We have to scan our thumb or retina to open any door in the building. You could only enter the loading dock door because the security system went down when the systems went offline."

"That was the only way for the kidnapper to get into the building then," Cal said, turning to her. "First, he had to make sure the systems went offline if he stood any chance of breaching the facility."

Bec's heart paused for a beat at the thought. "You're right. I didn't even think about how they got in here. Without the biometrics, we're sitting ducks."

"We've got you," Zac said without hesitation. "Our first order is to lock down all but one exit until Iris gets the biometrics up and running again. We'll keep a close eye on that exit, but in case of a fire, head to the loading bay if you can't reach the side door. We'll extract you from there."

"Got it," Iris said with a nod. "Time is slipping away from us. I should get to work."

"Agreed, and I need to get back to Secure Inc.," Cal said. "I'll turn it around as quickly as possible, but I expect to be gone at least six hours. Bec, is there somewhere in the area where I can rent four-wheelers or UTVs?"

"There are several places in Sinlis Park. We're between hunting seasons, so they should be easy to come by."

"I'll get Mina on that so the guys can get back and forth from here to town without taking the two we have." Cal reached into his pocket and pulled out a small button. "This is a panic button." He pushed it toward her. "We all wear one. Put it somewhere that's easy to activate but won't be accidentally pressed. It's waterproof, so wear it at all times. If you ever get in a situation where you need immediate assistance, press it. It's a GPS locator, so it's silent but tells us where you are."

"Got it," she said, swiping the button off the table and tucking it in her pocket.

"Are there sleeping accommodations here in the facility?" Cal asked, addressing her again.

"Not many," she said with a shake of her head. "I have

a small apartment where Iris can rest, but there isn't room for multiple people."

"What about the storage room off the loading dock?" Declan asked. "It's nearly empty, so there's room for several cots, which is all we'll need if we're running shifts."

"That would work," Bec agreed. "There's a bathroom and a decontamination shower just outside of that room as well. "There's a small break room with a microwave and fridge on that floor. There isn't much to cook with, though."

Cal chuckled. "We're all used to MREs when in the field. Food is the least of our worries." He pointed at Declan and Zac. "Head out and get those exits secured. We can't risk the kidnappers returning when we aren't prepared. Once I know who will be coming in to help you cover, I'll radio in. We'll bring the needed supplies for bedding down along with extra food."

"You got it, boss," Declan said. "Safe travels. Danger, out."

"Zulu, out." Zac saluted his boss and followed Declan, leaving just the three of them.

"Danger?" Bec asked.

Cal bit back a smile. "His call sign in the service. Let me reiterate that when I say don't call the police, I only mean if you can avoid it." He glanced between them. "If one of my men is hurt, the place goes up in flames or one of you is in trouble, then you call the police."

"Understood, boss," Iris said. "Not that it would matter. The police are so far away that by the time they arrived, we'd be dead anyway." Bec gasped, immediately noticing Iris's grimace. "Sorry. I should stop talking."

Bec shook her head as her shoulders slumped forward.

"Iris, you didn't say anything that isn't true. It just took me by surprise when you pointed it out."

Bec felt terrible that she'd upset Iris and made her feel she had to stop talking. That was the very last thing she wanted. The woman was captivating in her beauty, knowledge and matter-of-fact way of seeing life. She could appreciate someone who wasn't afraid to say it like it was, whether by choice or not. Life was short, and trying to dance around important subjects was never an effective way to communicate. However, what surprised her most about Iris was how quickly she calmed her with just one touch. A warm hand on her shoulder or brush of her fingers across hers, and Bec's heart rate slowed. While she didn't interact with anyone much, that wasn't the reason she was comforted by the woman's touch. Iris Knowles was intriguing. In any other scenario, she'd ask her out for dinner and drinks, but they were in a fight for their lives, so the last thing she could do was distract her from her job.

"We have a built-in system for fire suppression," Bec said to cover her momentary lapse into silence. "She's right about the police. Sinlis Park only has one full-time officer and one part-time, so the closest force that could help is over thirty minutes from here."

"Which is why I'll be setting up a command post in Sinlis Park," Cal said. "It keeps us within a few miles of the facility, allowing us to monitor everything closely. To do that, I need to get back to Secure Inc. Since the kidnapping occurred only a few hours ago, I'm confident that you're safe here with Declan and Zac. If you need anything, you know the protocols," he said to Iris, who nodded.

"Get after it then," he said, patting her shoulder. "Charlie, out."

He spun on his bootheel and strode from the room, leaving the two women facing each other. "That was a lot," Bec said as Iris ducked her head to stare at the table. "Do you need a breather?"

"I'm okay. I'd rather get started if that's okay with you."

"That's absolutely fine," Bec said, motioning her forward. "Where would you like to set up your machines? Let's avoid Dr. Hoerman's office for now. If we have to call the police, they'll want it untouched."

"I'd like to be wherever you are," Iris said, and Bec glanced behind her to catch Iris's eye for a second. "I get nervous in new environments and don't like to be alone until I know where everything is and—"

Bec turned and took her hands. "You're safe here with me, Iris. Please, don't feel you have to justify anything to me, okay? Just know you're safe, and I'm here to help you, whether you need coffee or have a question about the system."

Iris smiled and held her gaze momentarily, which she took as a solid win in her column. "Thank you, Bec. I appreciate that you don't think I'm weird like most people do. Well, not the people I work with, but everyone else."

"Sweetheart, it upsets me to know others make you feel that way. We're all different, but wouldn't this world be boring if we weren't? Now, we could pull one of the empty tables over to sit next to my desk. That way, as you work, you will also have easy access to my computer. Does that work for you?"

"That would be a good idea," Iris agreed, staring at

the floor again. "I'll call Declan to come move the table. My foot drop makes it hard to push things around."

"I got this," Bec said with a wink. "I can do the heavy lifting with this since you'll do the heavy lifting that matters."

Forcing herself to turn away from the woman who had charmed her so quickly, she prayed Iris had the skills to fix this mess before mankind suffered unimaginable pain and loss. She was betting on the quiet, unassuming woman who thought she didn't matter to prove just the opposite was true. Bec vowed to make sure Iris understood her worth, or she'd quite literally die trying.

Chapter Five

Iris pulled her hands from the keyboard and took her glasses off to rub her eyes. She'd been working on getting the containment and ventilation systems under Bec's control again by writing a workaround code for the malware. Ace still controlled the entire lab system, so she was confused about why they hadn't received a ransom request yet. He held all the cards and could demand anything he wanted, so why hadn't he? Why had he kidnapped Dr. Hoerman if he didn't plan to leverage him for money? Her biggest fear, that he would use him to access the virus, was still a real possibility. He could demand the virus and open the lab long enough for Bec to get Ignis Cerebri before meeting him with the deadly pathogen. She had been half convinced that two things were happening until Bec mentioned biometrics was the only way to get inside the facility. Ace and the kidnapper had to be working together or were one and the same, otherwise the kidnapper would never have gotten inside. Frustrated, she blew out a breath and tried to refocus. She had to keep working regardless of what he might do.

"How about a break?" Bec asked, setting a cup of coffee down in front of her. "You've been at this for hours."

Iris greedily picked up the coffee cup and took a long

gulp of the hot liquid. "Oh, that's good," she said with a sigh. "Thanks. If I don't finish this workaround soon, I'll need another gallon." She took another sip. "Is that caramel?"

"Yep," Bec said, sitting at her desk with a mug, too. "It's my guilty pleasure. I have it shipped in from a place in Wisconsin. I had it once at a hotel in Door County and have been a fan ever since."

"You don't get out much, do you?" Iris asked, and Bec chuckled. "I'm sorry. That wasn't meant sarcastically. Like, I meant, you don't get to go out much while working here, right?"

"I know what you meant," Bec promised, patting her leg and sending a tendril of heat into Iris's belly. She had known Bec less than twelve hours yet somehow, it felt like they'd been intimate partners for years. Something in Bec's touch told her she felt the same way. "And you're correct. I've been working here since May and haven't left the compound other than for a daily walk."

"Five months is a long time to be this secluded," Iris said. "Is that by choice?"

Bec's laughter filled the space, and Iris thought it was a lovely sound. It reminded her of Hannah Grace's laugh when she was on the swing on a sunny afternoon. "It's not a choice in the respect that I can come and go as I please. I could leave if I had to, but organizing that would be more effort than it was worth for an occasional outing. It was better to keep working on the vaccine since, as you know, the sooner the better when it comes to this virus."

A shudder racked Iris, but it wasn't from the cold. "The very idea of it is disconcerting. Especially knowing those systems are still under someone else's control." The idea was too much to bear, so Iris set her mug down and started typing again. "I keep telling myself he has to know that if he lets this virus go free, he's dead, too, right?"

"I've been telling myself the same thing, but we can't know that for certain. That said, he wouldn't know what we even housed here for viruses unless he hacked our system, which is entirely possible."

Iris paused her typing to glance at the woman next to her. "That's not true."

"What now?" Bec asked, setting the mug down. "What's not true?"

"That he has no way of knowing what's here. Have you ever googled this place?"

"I haven't needed to," Bec answered defensively.

Iris motioned at her phone with her chin. "Do it."

Bec reached for the phone, and Iris noticed her fingers shaking. After a few moments, she glanced up from her phone. "There's very little here other than Walter's interview with a science journal."

"Click it," Iris ordered with her fingers still tapping on her keyboard.

Bec was silent for several minutes before she inhaled sharply. "Nightmares are real, and one resides in my lab." With a heavy sigh, Bec tossed the phone onto the desk. "What was he thinking? He knows better than that!"

"It was a science journal. Maybe he thought no one else would see it?" Iris asked, her fingers still typing even as she spoke.

"I suppose that's possible, but he knows everything ends up on the internet. When was that dated?" She grabbed the phone again and checked the date. "April. I got here in May."

"Was there a head research scientist before you?" Iris asked, and Bec nodded. "Yes, but he didn't last long. I think he started in February but was gone by April. That was when I was hired."

"Do you know why he left?"

"I don't," she said with a shrug. "It could have been the isolation of the job, inability to work closely with Walter, or fear of the viruses themselves."

"Or did he get the information he wanted regarding the deadly viruses to leverage against the center?"

"I guess anything is possible," Bec agreed.

"Do you remember his name?"

"Yes. Samuel Gill."

Iris nodded as she typed. "When I finish this line of code, I need to call Secure Watch for my midnight check-in. We can give Mina his name, and she can look into him while we keep working."

Bec reached over and put her hand on Iris's shoulder. "You have to sleep, Iris."

"I'll sleep when this is over," Iris said, not breaking pace. "Or at least once I get the most important functions under our control again."

"What if you can't?"

"Then I'll die trying." She stopped looking at the computer long enough to glance at the woman beside her. She read the terror in her eyes and held her gaze longer than anyone she ever had before. "How do you do that?"

"Do what, Iris?"

"Make it so easy for me to make eye contact."

"I can't answer that question. Only you can. It might

be easier for you to answer this question. Why do you struggle to maintain eye contact with others?"

"Judgment," she said without hesitation. "I'm always worried they're going to judge me."

"Then maybe the answer to your first question is that you aren't worried I'll judge you."

"I'm not," she agreed immediately. "You already said you wouldn't."

"And you believed that without even knowing me."

"I'm good at reading people. Ever since my accident, I could always tell when someone was silently judging me. Teachers. Friends. Employers."

"My guess is you don't feel judged at Secure Watch?"

"Nope," she agreed. "But I still struggle with eye contact there. It's easier, but not like with you."

"Are you worried that your TBI might affect your employment?"

"It's always a worry. Sometimes, I feel like a burden to Mina and Cal, so I try not to make waves. That was the only reason I planned to come here when Mina asked. Until I saw you on the screen for the first time. You were so beautiful, and when you spoke, your voice calmed my racing heart and helped it beat normally again. Ugh. Why am I like this? I'm going to stop talking now."

Bec chuckled and patted her shoulder. "Never feel like you can't be honest with me, Iris. I'm grateful you're here, no matter how that decision happened. It's nice knowing Declan and Zac have my back with security, but knowing I'm not alone inside the lab is everything right now. I'm terrified and exhausted, but you're making it easier by being here."

Iris smiled but didn't say anything more as she typed.

Before she replied, she wanted to think about what Bec said to decide how it made her feel. She'd learned to take time to think over interactions with new people before she said something she couldn't take back. Especially in high-stress situations like they were in tonight. They'd been working for hours, and it was late, but she couldn't rest until she had some control over the lab.

"Do you know of anyone with a grudge against you, Dr. Hoerman or the center?" Iris asked instead.

"Other than past scientists, no. I wouldn't know if they had issues with the center since I never met them."

"Other scientists had grudges against him?" Iris asked, surprise in her tone.

"It's possible," Bec said with a shoulder shrug. "None of them lasted long, but I don't know the circumstances. I was simply saying that I only know the names of the last few scientists who worked here. Anything else was information I didn't need."

"Would Dr. Hoerman have information on former employees in his office?"

"I'm sure the names of the past scientists would be in a file somewhere, sure," Bec answered. "Without him here, I wouldn't know if they had any issues with the center, though."

"If you can find their names, Mina could look into them, if nothing else," Iris said just as her tablet started to ring. "Speaking of Mina." She tore her hands from the keypad and grabbed the tablet, hitting the answer button. "Secure Watch, India."

"Secure Watch, Whiskey," Mina replied before the camera flipped on. Mina sat at her desk in her private office. "Iris. How are you holding up?"

"Tired, but still working," she answered, glancing at Bec and motioning her closer. "Have you guys found anything regarding Ace or Dr. Hoerman?"

"Nothing so far," Mina said. "But Cal just got to a motel at Sinlis Park to set up an outpost station for us about an hour ago."

"More likely the only motel," Bec said, and Mina laughed.

"You're not kidding, but it's the closest we could get without being obvious. Have you heard anything more from Ace?"

"I would have called you instantly if he'd contacted us," Iris said. "But Bec did think of something you might be able to help us with."

"Hit me," Mina said, grabbing her pen and notebook, so Iris motioned for Bec to fill her in.

"The last scientist to work here before me only lasted a few months. I don't know why that is, but Iris thought it might be important."

"That's absolutely worth a little investigating on my end. What was his name?"

"Samuel Gill. I don't know anything more than that about him, but he was a cell, molecular and disease biologist like me, so there can't be many of those in the country with the same name."

"That should narrow it down," Mina agreed. "Anyone else?"

"We were just talking about that," Iris said. "I suggested that she go through Dr. Hoerman's files and see if anyone else left after such a short period of working here."

"I wasn't sure it would apply," Bec jumped in. "I don't

know any of them or their circumstances for leaving, so it could be a wild-goose chase."

"Could be," Mina agreed. "But Iris is correct. It's important to run a background check on everyone who used to work there just like we did on you and Walter."

"You ran a background on me?"

"Before you get onto the big screen, you're vetted," Mina answered. "We don't play at Secure Watch, but your circumstances were dire enough to bring in the team while still checking you out."

"That's fair," Bec said. "I think it would be a waste of time, though. Ignis Cerebri hasn't been in the facility for that long."

"Be that as it may, you've always had deadly viruses and pathogens there, correct?" Mina asked, and Bec nodded. "Then it stands to reason Ace could be any scientist who previously worked there. They may not know about Ignis Cerebri, but they know you don't want anything inside that lab to escape or fall into the wrong hands."

"I hadn't thought of it that way, but you're right. We can only hope and pray they don't know Ignis Cerebri is here."

"Do you have access to Walter's personnel files?"

"Sort of. He keeps them in a file cabinet in his office, but he has the key on his belt. Cal also told me not to mess with anything in his office until we can bring the police in on this."

"A key is no problem. Zac can open a file cabinet in his sleep. You have gloves there?" Bec nodded as Mina smiled. "Even though your prints are already on everything in that lab, wear gloves and touch only the cabinet. Grab any and all files for the employees who quit or were fired. Especially anyone who wasn't a scientist."

"Why?" Iris asked.

"Scientists usually aren't big tech people," Mina answered, and Bec pointed at the screen.

"True that. We can do what we need to do for our research and work, but what we're dealing with here is a level unlike anything I could ever think up, much less know how to write a program to take control of an entire system."

Mina nodded. "The faster you can get the information, the better. Iris, I would like you to record it from start to finish. We want to document anything we do in his office that requires breaking and entering to prove it was necessary during the course of the investigation."

"I still think we need to call the police," Bec said, biting her lip. "The only person who will pay for waiting will be me."

"While I would normally agree with you, I can't in this instance. If we bring in the cops, they'll take over and prevent Iris from getting her work done. Not to mention, that also puts more people in the middle of Armageddon. We can't take our eyes off the prize until the facility has been secured again and there's no risk of those pathogens finding their way out the door. After that, we'll call the police, FBI and any other three-letter organization we need to find this guy."

"What if it's too late for Walter?" Bec asked, and Iris heard the tremble in her words. Her heart hurt to know Bec was going through this, and there was nothing she could do to help other than keep mashing away on the keys and pray she could turn this around for them. Well, there was one other thing she could do, so she did it. She slid her hand over Bec's knee and gently squeezed it to let her know she was there for her.

"It could already be too late for Walter, but it's not too late for the rest of the world. I know that's a hard pill to swallow when your friend is in danger, but this is a rock and a hard place situation if I've ever seen one. Give Iris twenty-four hours to get the place locked down safely. We'll bring in the authorities if we haven't heard from Ace by then. My gut says Walter is still alive. Ace isn't done with us, and he'll need Walter alive as a bargaining chip if he hopes to get any money out of the facility. There was no other reason to storm in and take him. He could be traveling to a different state or letting you sweat for a while, so you're more apt to do what he demands when he reaches out. Either way, we stay the course until we hear from him."

Bec nodded several times before she straightened her spine. "You're right. I called you guys in to help, so I need to trust what you're telling me to do. If I'm left holding the bag and go to prison at the end of this, it will be worth it as long as no one dies a horrible death due to one of the pathogens in this facility."

Iris squeezed Bec's knee again. "Cal and Mina won't let that happen. Neither will I."

"She's right," Mina said with a smile. "We got you. Trust the process and get me those names ASAP. I'll radio Zac to head in and open the cabinet for you now. Keep me abreast of anything that comes in from Ace or if you get the systems back online."

"Will do," Iris said without letting go of Bec's knee. "India, out."

The screen went blank, and Bec's shoulders sank the moment they were alone again. "I don't feel good about this, Iris, but I'll do it if we can save Walter."

"I'm sure he would want you to do anything you can think of to help him," Iris said, turning her chair and taking Bec's hand. "Remember that Secure Inc. won't let you get caught up in this mess. That's why you hired us to help. We wouldn't have taken the case if we didn't think we could handle it."

Bec blew out a breath and nodded. "Right. I need to remember to trust you."

"You trust me?"

"From the moment Cal introduced you," she said, her smile small as she dropped her gaze to their hands. "I just hope you trust me, too."

"I wouldn't be holding your hand if I didn't," Iris said before she grimaced. "Sorry—"

Bec put her finger to Iris's lips. "Remember that you can be yourself here without apologizing for it. I hate that people in your past made you feel like you had to, but not with me, okay?"

Iris forced herself to hold Bec's gaze for several seconds, and she found herself lost in her eyes for a beat longer than she had expected before she answered. "Okay. I'll probably forget more than I remember, though."

"Then I'll keep reminding you until it comes naturally," Bec said with a wink. "Why did you call yourself India on the call with Mina?"

"Oh, I should tell you about that. Secure Inc. uses code names when contacting another team member on assignment. Mina is Whiskey because her real name is Wilhemina. Cal is Charlie. I'm India."

"Declan is Danger," Bec said, laughing as though she finally understood the situation.

"Yes, and while he can't say what he did for the army, Danger was his call sign. Essentially, if a team member were ever to use something other than their code name, we would know they're in trouble and need help."

"That's incredibly smart. It keeps the majority of the team safe and gets help to the team member in trouble without showing your hand."

"Secure One, Zulu."

"Case in point," Iris said, spinning in her chair to see Zac standing in the lab.

They both stood, and while Bec explained to Zac what they needed and why, Iris turned to grab her tablet to record the encounter. She used that short minute to take a deep breath and remind herself that she had one job to do here. She couldn't let her desire to know more about the beautiful and engaging scientist beside her keep her from doing it. With her resolve set, she followed them to the office, but for the life of her, she couldn't convince herself there wasn't a way to do both.

Chapter Six

The file cabinet held a few employee files but nothing recent, which surprised Bec. "It isn't like Walter not to have files on previous employees."

"Maybe he put them on the computer?" Iris asked after she stopped recording. "We didn't see one for Samuel Gill, so maybe he moved everything to digital files to make space?"

"It's possible, but he's not super techy. I can barely get him to work with the programs we use for the labs."

"This wouldn't be hard, though," she said, motioning at the few files on the desk. "With a scanner, he could easily upload them. Even your basic idiot can make a folder on their computer."

Iris slapped a hand over her mouth, and Bec stopped her before she could apologize. "Don't say you're sorry. You're correct. Walter is good with scanners and does basic tasks with a computer, but we can't look at his laptop, which hampers us in knowing if that's where the files are."

"We have records for the three years before this one, right?" Iris asked, and Bec nodded. "Let's send Mina those names. She'll want to do a deep dive into each person, and we have five people for her to track down besides Samuel. That will take them a few days, and if nothing turns up, at least we tried. It seems like an especially high turnover rate, but I could be wrong for a job like this."

"It is high," Bec said, falling into her desk chair after they left Walter's office. "After working here for five months, I may know why."

"People are scared of the viruses? I know I am." Iris bit her lip as her gaze strayed to the labs.

Bec reached out and squeezed her knee. "Don't let the fear in. If you let the fear in, it makes it impossible to get anything done. Keep your eyes on me and your head in the game."

"Right," she said with a nod. "Eyes on you. That's hard for me, but you make it easier." She cleared her throat as though to gloss over that admittance. "Why do you think people keep quitting the lab?"

"Fear isn't one of them," Bec said with a shake of her head. "If they accepted a position here, they already knew what kind of work was required. I suspect the reason no one lasts long is twofold. The first is the isolation. It's lonely out here, and if you aren't dedicated to the job or took it for a reason that wasn't your own, you won't last."

"You must have a good reason if you've lasted long enough to make a vaccine."

"It's purely selfish," Bec admitted. "If I could research and implement a vaccine for something like Ignis Cerebri, it would mean I could write my own ticket to work anywhere in the world."

"That makes all of this isolation worth it?" Iris asked, the fatigue showing as each minute ticked away.

"Well, before Ace hit, the answer was yes. I hoped to get into a university somewhere, but now I'll just be happy to get out alive."

"You and me both," Iris agreed. "What's the second reason?"

"The management."

"Dr. Hoerman isn't a good manager?"

"Not great," Bec admitted with a mirthless chuckle. "Super nice guy, but if you need direction or questions answered promptly, you won't get them from him."

"Is his job to manage?"

"Indirectly," Bec said, hoping to explain it better. "He's the project manager, meaning he finds the projects people need done, organizes, brings them in and implements them."

"That sounds like a manager to me."

Bec motioned at her. "Me, too, but he believes that if we're qualified to get the job as head scientist, we're his equal. He's not wrong—however, he knows the project parameters better than we do since he's the intake guy."

"So if he doesn't communicate the parameters well, that leaves you frustrated," Iris deduced and Bec pointed at her in agreement. "Are there other scientists working here?"

"Since Ignis is here, we only have one lab tech right now. Walter and I decided the fewer people in the lab with this virus, the better."

"Where is the lab tech now? Did he quit?"

"No, his name is Zafar. He's on vacation. He's scheduled to be out for another week. I'd try to call him, but he's at a wedding in Poland. I'd rather wait and see if we can get a handle on this first."

"Agreed. Does Mina have his information to do a background check?"

"Yes. I gave her that when we first connected."

Iris rubbed the bridge of her nose and pushed her tablet toward Bec. "Would you send Mina the information while I get back to work on the system?"

"No," Bec said, pushing the tablet back toward her. "It's 3:00 a.m., and we're both exhausted. Mina is in bed and won't get the message anyway. We need to rest before we do anything else."

"No time to rest," Iris said, shaking her head adamantly. "We don't know what Ace is going to do next. We must get control of this place."

Bec squeezed Iris's shoulder while she ducked her head until she found the woman's eyes. "I trust you, Iris, with my life, but I also know how working tired can be more dangerous than taking a few hours to rest and then coming back to it."

"Secure One, Danger." They both jumped and turned to see Declan standing in the hallway. "Sorry, I didn't mean to scare you, but she's right. I was leaving the break room to bed down for a few hours of sleep when I overheard the discussion. Per Cal's instructions, you are to get a few hours of sleep each day," he said, lowering his brow at Iris. "You've been up for twenty hours. It's time to grab a couple of hours' rest so you can return refreshed. Otherwise, you're just spinning your wheels."

Iris sighed heavily. "Fine, but two hours. That's it."

Declan nodded once. "I can deal with that. Zac and I will start rotating shifts since Cal sent Mack and Efren over to cover. If you need us, we're on the loading dock."

"Got it. Thanks, Declan," Bec said, standing and holding her hand out for Iris. She wasn't sure if the woman would take it, but she yearned for that connection again. When Iris's warm, soft skin slid across her palm, she had to take a deep breath to slow her racing heart.

"Will you show me where the loading dock is?" Iris asked as Bec led her through the cavernous workspace and into the hallway.

"You're not going to sleep on the loading dock. You'll sleep in my apartment, where it's safe and comfortable."

"But, no. I'm supposed to sleep with the team."

Bec paused and turned back to the beautiful woman just as Iris pushed her glasses up her adorable pixie nose with her free hand. Rather than argue further, she snapped the walkie-talkie off her belt and pushed the button. "Declan?"

"This is Zac," the voice said, and Iris huffed but didn't say anything.

"Iris insists she should sleep with the team on the loading dock. I think she should be squirreled away safely in my apartment. What's your opinion?" She released the button and raised a brow at the woman across from her, who now had her hand on her hip even if she was staring over her shoulder at the wall beyond them. Bec couldn't decide if it made her look sassy, sexy or angry.

"If she can sleep in your apartment, that would be ideal," Zac responded. "I'd rather she wasn't this close to the action if something goes down outside."

"You got it," Bec said, releasing the button with a satisfied smile.

"Okay," Iris said with a huff. "But I'd be fine on the loading dock."

"Maybe, but this way, I can keep an eye on you. Something tells me if I let my guard down, you'll be back at that computer typing away."

When they stepped onto the elevator, Iris's smirk told her that was her plan to a T.

IRIS GLANCED AROUND the small apartment while Bec was in the shower. Using the word *apartment* was a stretch, if she was honest. It was the size of a hotel room with a queen-size bed, a small kitchenette, a two-person table and a nightstand. The bathroom off the main space was small but functional. Iris still couldn't imagine working and living here day after day without a change of scenery. Her room at Secure Inc. was small, but she had the entire building and grounds to roam whenever she needed a break.

Bec walked into the room wearing lounge clothes that in no way showed off her physique but were still far more alluring than her white lab coat. Iris dropped her gaze rather than continue to stare. "Oh good, you got the bed turned down," Bec said, rubbing lotion into her hands. "I was hoping you'd make yourself at home."

"I made tea," Iris said, pointing at the two mugs on the table. "It's not my favorite, but coffee before bed won't work so well."

"I couldn't agree more." Bec offered her a tired smile.

Iris walked to her and pushed her hair back off her face to check the cuts that peppered her skin from the attack. "I'm so sorry you went through that this morning. Are you sure you don't need a doctor? Are you having any symptoms of a concussion?"

"I'm fine," Bec promised, taking her hand. "The glass cut my face, but I never hit my head."

Her sleeve slipped down from her wrist when she grasped Iris's hand and revealed what she'd been hiding under the lab coat. Iris's gasp was loud in the room. "You're not fine, Bec. Why didn't you show this to someone? What happened?"

Iris inspected her arm. It was red, blistered and covered in gashes of different depths.

"I don't know what happened, if I'm honest. I think I threw my arm up to protect my face and it got hit with hot shrapnel. When I wrapped it earlier while waiting for you guys to arrive, it wasn't red and blistered yet. I thought I'd let it breathe while we were sleeping."

Iris bit her lip as she stared at the wounded flesh. "That's probably not smart. You could get an infection, or what about tetanus or something? You should probably go to the hospital. I need to call Cal to take you to the hospital. This isn't good. This is really not good." Her breathing was at a fever pitch now, and her vision had gone tunnel as she stared at the damaged skin.

The next thing she knew, she was sitting on the bed, and Bec was kneeling before her. "Take some deep breaths, Iris." She coached her by breathing with her until Iris stopped shaking and sound filtered back into her ears.

"That was embarrassing," she said, staring at the floor. "I'm sorry for freaking out. It happens more than usual when I'm stressed out."

Bec tipped her chin up to face her. She didn't force her to hold her gaze and didn't say anything when Iris couldn't. "Don't apologize for caring, Iris. I don't know who made you feel like you have to stare at the floor rather than hold your head high, but here in my apartment, you can be unapologetically you without hanging your head in shame, okay?"

"That's not why," she said, staring over her shoulder at the wall. "It's easier to talk to people when I don't have to look at them. My brain works better that way."

"To a degree, I believe that," Bec said. "But I think you started doing it when you realized that your bluntness, as you put it, can embarrass you or others, so staring at the floor means you don't have to see the judgment on others' faces."

Iris didn't want to admit she was right, so she didn't answer. "I think you should cover your arm with something before sleeping. It would be bad if you scratched it accidentally in your sleep. I know you're like a doctor and everything, so it's fine if you don't want to do that. As my mama always said, I see things very literally and with too much common sense, so I'm probably wrong."

"I am a doctor, but not a medical one. I hadn't thought of your point about scratching it in my sleep. Getting an infection wouldn't be convenient right now, so I'll wrap it in gauze."

Iris nodded just as a yawn overtook her. She covered her mouth with her hand, apologizing for being rude.

"Don't apologize. We've had one hell of a day. Go ahead and get comfortable while I wrap my arm, and then we can shut down the lights for a few hours."

"If you tell me where to find a sleeping bag or extra blankets, I'll make my bed."

"What do you want those for?"

Iris glanced down at the floor and back to her momentarily. “It’s no problem. I can sleep on the floor without a bag. Do you have an extra pillow?”

“You’re not sleeping on the floor,” Bec said with a chuckle as she motioned her to the head of the bed. “You have the most important job in the place now. That means you’re sleeping in the bed.”

Bec pulled the blankets around Iris and then grasped the bows of her glasses to slide them off. There was something evocative about the sensation of the metal leaving her face when it wasn’t of her own volition. She was used to doing everything for herself, and having someone care for her was a foreign sensation. “Where are you going to sleep?”

Bec turned back to her, wearing a nervous smile. “Right next to you. I’ll keep you safe, Iris.”

Then she disappeared into the bathroom, leaving Iris to decide if sharing a bed with the beautiful scientist was more dangerous to her health than the unchecked pathogens in the lab above their heads.

Chapter Seven

Iris's fingers flew across the keyboard the second they hit the keys. She had fallen asleep before Bec had returned from the bathroom, but when she woke, to say she was disoriented was an understatement. Her anxiety was not being kind, but she'd managed to get her braces on and get out of bed without waking Bec. They had shared a bed, and while it had been entirely innocent, a large part of her wanted it to be so much more.

Bec hadn't come out and said she was gay, but she didn't have to for Iris to know. For her, it came down to their connection when their skin touched. The moment their eyes met, she knew. That was saying a lot for someone who struggled with connecting. When Bec was in the shower, she also noticed a magnet on her fridge for Out to Innovate, an organization for LGBTQ+ scientists and technical professionals. She recognized it because she'd been a member for years.

Since Bec didn't know she was also a member, she'd keep it that way. Mostly because she was struggling with how kind and understanding Bec was about her TBI. Sure, everyone at Secure Inc. was kind and patient, but they worked together every day. This was different. She and Bec had barely met before Bec immediately reassured her she belonged. She accepted her and allowed her to take up space in a way that didn't result in judgment or sarcastic comments despite her overreaction to several situations. It usually took months or years for people to get comfortable with her and how her brain worked. Sometimes, people were never comfortable with who she was despite knowing she couldn't change it. She'd experienced that with friends and girlfriends enough times over the years that she tended to keep to herself now. That was why she enjoyed working at Secure Watch. The core team stayed the same, making it easier for her to relax and be confident there without worrying about being judged.

No one ever questioned her skills on the job, and she knew she was better at her job than many in her field, but that was because of how her brain worked. The most challenging part was proving herself to others when they couldn't see past her diagnoses. It wasn't an untold story for neurodivergent people. No matter how much people were educated about neurodiversity, there would always be a level of prejudice against them for something outside of their control. But then, that was a problem for marginalized communities as a whole. She couldn't fix that by herself, unlike the code she was writing to get the lab back under her control. She was close. She could feel it in her fingers with each new line of code she wrote.

A glance at the clock told her it had been several hours since she'd left Bec's apartment. That wasn't a big surprise. If there was one thing she could get lost in, it was her work. Truthfully, she worried Bec would be upset that she got up and left, but she also didn't want to wake her after so few hours of sleep. After the day Bec had yesterday, she needed rest, especially with the injury to her arm. As soon as Iris finished the code, she planned to text Cal to ask him if he had brought Selina from Secure Inc. with him. Selina was a nurse who usually traveled with them on assignment. Iris wasn't sure if this qualified since Cal wanted to keep as many people out of the fallout zone as possible, but she suspected Selina wouldn't give him a choice. He needed a medical professional on-site for every case, so she hoped she was right. She wanted her to look at Bec's arm and treat it if need be. The blisters would pop sooner rather than later, and the last thing she needed was an infection that required her to leave the facility. Without Bec here, they would have to turn this over to the police, which could get them all killed.

Not that Iris thought she was all that when it came to fixing this situation, but she knew this was not the kind of place that could be left unattended, or worse yet, have the police bring someone in to break into the labs. The very idea made her shudder, and she forced her fingers to move faster as her eyes tried to track the lines on the screen, but the hours she'd already put in were catching up to her.

"Come on, come on," she chanted, finishing the last line and gingerly pressing the return key as the elevator door dinged.

She momentarily lifted her gaze from the keyboard and waited for something to happen, though she had no idea what to expect.

Bec walked into the room carrying two cups of coffee just as a whirring started above their heads. Iris stood up. "What is that? It just came on!"

Bec set the mugs on the table and swiveled toward Iris. She ran to her with a whoop and threw her arms around her while jumping up and down. "You did it! That's the ventilation system!"

"You mean it's working?" Iris asked when Bec released her.

"Yes!" She motioned her toward a lab door. "Look." Iris peered into the room where papers fluttered on a table. "You did it!"

"Okay, so the ventilation system is working, but the labs don't have the lights on over the doors," Iris said, pointing above them.

"Those lights indicate lab access and the containment system, not the ventilation system. The lights won't come on until the containment system is working again—at least, I think that's what will happen. They may be working, but I have no way to know when I can't control the system from here."

"Are the viruses just floating around in there now that I put the vents back on?"

"No," Bec assured her, hands out to keep her calm. "That's not how it works. The viruses are safely locked up right now."

"If that's the case, why the big deal then?"

"Because Ace could release them if he controls the containment system. Now that you have the ventilation system back, the filters in the vents will be working again. If anything is released, it should get trapped before it gets vented out of the facility. We don't know how long Ignis Cerebri stays alive in the air. All we know is, once inhaled by the primary case, it will spread like wildfire."

"Are there other viruses here, too?"

"Many," Bec agreed, walking with Iris back to the desks. "Those are viruses and bacteria that we know more about, though. Releasing them could be dangerous, but when you have an unknown like Ignis Cerebri, that's your focus. I have seen what it can do to animals. We don't want it set loose on the population."

Iris lowered herself back to the chair. "I need to get the containment system under our control then. Right now."

"If you can do that, the world will be safe from anything behind those doors while we wait for Ace to contact us."

Forcing herself up again, Iris eyed the hallway. "I should let the team know the ventilation system is secured."

"We will," Bec said, taking her hand. "Take a deep breath first." Iris inhaled with her, and then Bec patted her back.

"What are you doing?"

"I'm giving you a pat on the back for getting that system under our control again. I know it's your job, but it wasn't easy, and you deserve recognition for it."

"It was a lot," Iris agreed. "What I learned can be applied to the next system, too, which hopefully means it won't take me as long to get the containment system back online. Whoever this Ace guy is, he's talented in a diabolical way, but he doesn't seem to be watching his code closely, which has been working in my favor. Regardless, we need to put him behind bars."

"We will," Bec assured her, squeezing her hand. "Thanks in no small part to you."

"There's a lot left to do, Bec," Iris said, wanting to

pull away but transfixed by the trust in her big, beautiful brown eyes. "We can't get ahead of ourselves."

"I know, but I also know you never stop to consider how imperative your skills are in many people's lives."

Iris shrugged as though she was unbothered by the compliment when it meant everything to hear. She didn't know how to show that or what to say, though.

"I suspect it's hard for you to accept compliments, and that's okay, but I want you to know how much I appreciate you."

"And I appreciate how kind you are to me, Bec. I'm not used to that. You look beautiful today. Not that you didn't yesterday, I just meant—"

Bec's finger came down on her lips, forcing her to resist the urge to kiss it. "You just meant that yesterday I was tired and had been through a lot."

Iris nodded until Bec dropped her finger. "That's what I meant. How is your arm?"

"Sore," she admitted. "I'll keep an eye on it."

Iris snapped her fingers. "That reminds me of something I have to ask Cal. We need to find the team, update them and then return to the code."

"Yes, Captain!" Bec said, standing straight with a wink. "Let's take our coffee to go."

They grabbed their coffee cups and headed for the elevator just as it dinged, and the doors slid open. Zac ran out but stopped when he saw them.

"You're okay."

"Of course," Iris answered. "Why wouldn't I be?"

"We heard whirring from the loading dock but couldn't raise you on the walkie-talkie."

Her heart rate picked up speed when she realized her

mistake. “Oh no,” she whispered, staring at the ground. “I left it in the apartment this morning. It was charging last night, and then I forgot about it. I don’t usually have them. See, this is why I can’t be trusted! Cal’s going to be so mad. He’s going to convince Mina to fire me!”

Chapter Eight

Zac held his hands out for calm, but she didn't feel that way. "Iris, no," he said. "No one is mad. We were just worried."

"But you don't know that," she whispered, walking backward until she bumped into Bec. She nearly tipped over until Bec grasped her waist and held her in place. She was trembling and embarrassed, knowing her misstep had caused confusion and concern for the team.

"Iris, take a deep breath," Bec instructed. "Focus on my words. Breathe in quickly twice and back out slowly."

Iris followed her instructions, trying to keep from spiraling into all the situations that could arise from her inability to remember things outside her regular routine. She could write code all day and never forget a character, but other tasks—things like what to get at the store or remembering she needed to carry the walkie-talkie around—were more difficult. When she started living independently, she needed notes to remind her of every task, but she no longer needed to depend on them as she used to. "I don't usually have one and forgot to put a note on my phone the way I usually do when I have to remember something important."

"Why didn't you call her phone?" Bec asked, and Zac smacked himself in the forehead.

"Never even thought of it. That's on me. I'm sorry for upsetting you, Iris. I should have texted you. We're used to using the walkies, so I didn't think about it."

Bec patted Iris's waist before she spoke. "Listen, everyone here is under a lot of stress and pressure, so let's make sure we give ourselves and each other a little bit of grace, okay?"

"Secure One, Charlie, and I couldn't agree more," a voice said from behind them, and they all jumped to see Cal standing there with several others.

"Cal. When did you get here?" Iris asked, her voice steady now that Bec had her arm around her.

"We took the stairs," he answered, motioning behind him.

"I got the ventilation system going again," she said in response, wanting him to know she may have screwed up one thing, but she was still doing her job. "Bec said that's important but not as important as the containment system, so I'll do that next."

Cal stepped forward and patted her shoulder. "I'm proud of you, Iris. Way to go! I knew you were the right woman for the job."

"But I messed up and—" Bec squeezed her waist, and she stopped speaking, taking a deep breath rather than continuing.

"You forgot the walkie, which is no big deal," Cal assured her. "If I know you, and I do, you didn't sleep much and then got up early to get back to work on the system."

"Yes, sir," Iris answered, glancing up to read his face. He didn't look upset, which was a relief. That was when she noticed Selina in the group. "Selina!" She ran and hugged her, which was not an uncommon reaction for her as they had become good friends since she started working at Secure Watch. She was worried about Bec's arm and was glad she'd come with Cal this morning.

"Hi, Iris," Selina said with a pat on her back. "Are you feeling okay?"

"Yes, but Bec got hurt more than she said yesterday. Could you look at her arm? It's burned."

"Burned?" Selina asked, glancing at Bec.

"There are some blisters. I don't know what happened. I do remember it was the arm I threw up to cover my face."

"Stun grenades can cause burns," Cal said. "The heat of the blast can heat things in its way. Like this metal table."

Bec's lips drew into a thin line. "It's possible that I touched one of these tables when disoriented."

"I'll look at it once we're finished with the update," Selina promised.

"Iris was just telling Zac that she got the ventilation system working again," Bec said, motioning toward her. "Thank God for that."

"But then Bec told me if I don't get the containment system online, Ace could release all kinds of things, so it wasn't that great of an accomplishment."

"Wrong," Cal said, his brow dipping. "Any system you can get back is an accomplishment. We can't protect the world if we don't protect this facility."

Bec nodded once. "She's had less than three hours of sleep but still got this far. I know she can get the containment online, too."

"What's left after that?" Cal asked, glancing between them.

"Nothing that could kill anyone," Bec answered simply. “But if she can get the lab door function back, at least I could lock things down further inside the main lab to protect everyone were we forced to abandon the facility.”

“That’s what we do then,” Cal said. “Iris, how long do you think before you get the containment system online?”

“If I apply what I learned with the ventilation system, and assuming Ace isn’t aware that I’ve messed with his code, which I don’t think he is, I should be able to do it in two hours. I have to write a workaround for his code and then protect it, so he doesn’t kill it again.”

Cal’s nod was tight. “Once you have the containment system live, I want you to rest. While Bec is correct that we want to protect everyone from what’s inside those labs, it can’t be at your expense.”

“I’ll grab a few hours and then get back at it. I’ll feel better once I know Bec can protect the world from that nasty virus.”

“I want to know why we haven’t heard from Ace yet,” Bec said, glancing between the team. “He kidnapped Walter almost twenty-four hours ago. Why do that if you aren’t going to ask for ransom?”

“A question I’ve asked myself, but this isn’t unheard of,” Selina said. “Sometimes people are kidnapped, and it’s days or even weeks before a ransom is demanded.”

“They’re letting us sweat,” Iris said, her gaze on the table. “If we think he has control of everything and also the head scientist of the lab, the one person who can fix anything, then we’re more likely to cooperate with him.”

“That’s a possible scenario,” Cal agreed.

“Walter isn’t the head scientist,” Bec interjected. “He’s a scientist, but an administrator-level scientist at this point. He’s near retirement and hasn’t worked in a lab for decades. He has nothing to do with the pathogens other than to write the proposals and accept the assignments. Ace should have taken me if he wanted that kind of bargaining chip."

"Would the general public know that?" Iris asked, peeking at her as Bec shook her head.

"Probably not. It would be an assumption of someone unfamiliar with the way places like this are run that he was the one to take."

"That was Ace's first mistake," Iris said with a shrug. "His second was underestimating your ability to think on your feet and bring in the firepower needed to handle this situation."

"Couldn't have said it better myself," Cal agreed with a chuckle. "While you're working on the code, we'll tighten our security plan and prepare exit strategies should we need them. Selina, join us downstairs when you're done checking Bec's arm?"

"It's fine, really," Bec said, holding up her hands. "I can manage it."

"If it's blistered, then I disagree," Selina said. "That means the burn is at least second-degree and will need special cream and care until it heals so you don't get an infection. I'll check it every day while I'm here. I'll grab my medic bag and meet you in your apartment."

Selina headed to the elevator as Bec grinned sheepishly at Iris. "I guess she told me." That got a snort from Iris. "She can do her thing with it, and then I'm going to make some breakfast and bring it up here for you to eat while you work. You'll be okay while I'm gone?"

"Yes," Iris said with a nod. "I'm not afraid to be alone. I've been alone all my life."

The look on Bec's face before she headed toward the stairs told Iris that it made her sad, and she felt terrible for doing that to her. It wasn't her intention, but she didn't know how to do anything but tell the truth. Sometimes, like right now, it would be easier if she could tell a little white lie now and again.

"Shouldn't have said that," Iris said when she was gone. "Now she's going to feel sorry for me, which I don't want."

"Bec doesn't strike me as the type to feel sorry for anyone, Iris," Cal soothed. "Let's stay on track. Do you need Mina's help with anything? She's waiting in the wings if you do."

"Is she still running down the information on the scientists we gave her last night?"

"Yes, that's her plan for this morning, but she can drop that at a moment's notice if you need help with something."

Iris nodded and blew out a breath as she rubbed her forehead. "Once I get the critical parts of the lab running again, I'll search Ace's code for a signature."

"Signature?"

"Usually, coders who spend time on the dark web or those with God complexes like Ace will have a signature. Something they do every time they code that makes them feel superior. It's usually how they write a specific tag or start the first part of a line," she explained, alternating her gaze between him and the poster on the wall. It was about pathogens and how they travel between people. "I hope to send some lines of code to Mina. If Ace is familiar to the community, we'll know quickly. It's faster for her to run that down while I keep working on protecting the system here."

"You have the support of all of Secure Inc.," Cal assured her. "I know you can do this, so I'll let you get back to it, but Iris?" he asked, and she shifted her gaze to his. "I never knew you had such beautiful eyes."

"Sir?" she asked, tipping her head in confusion.

"That was the first time you made eye contact for over three seconds. Thank you for trusting me."

She lifted her head and held it high, even if she was staring at the poster again. She nodded. "It's not that I didn't trust you."

"It's that you couldn't show me," Cal said. "I've always understood that, and I accept you no matter what. You'll see that's true of others if you give them the benefit of the doubt."

"In time, I suppose that will get easier," she agreed. "For now, I better get back to my work so we don't feel like we're watching the clock tick down on a bomb we can't disarm."

"Couldn't have said that better myself. I'll have Selina bring you the walkie-talkie when she's done helping Bec. You know where to find us if you need anything?"

When she nodded, he strolled from the room, whistling like they weren't fighting for their lives.

Chapter Nine

Bec kept her eyes glued to her arm as Selina unwrapped the gauze. She'd lied to Iris when she said it was fine and that she could handle it herself. When she got up this morning, it ached like nothing had before. She hadn't the nerve to take the bandage off it, so she was glad Selina had arrived with Cal.

"Do you see these red streaks here?" Selina asked, motioning at the spot above the gauze, and Bec nodded. "That's what we call lymphangitis. It means your arm is already infected. The streaks are infection of the channels going toward the lymph nodes in your armpit."

"When you saw that, you knew I couldn't handle it alone," Bec finished.

"I didn't want to alarm Iris, so I didn't say anything, but that's correct."

Bec hissed when she pulled the gauze off the wound. As soon as the air hit it, it told her the skin was indeed burned.

"Sorry," Selina said, glancing back at her as she tossed the gauze in the garbage. "The good news is, my bag is fully stocked with burn cream and antibiotics, so we'll have it fixed up in no time. That said, I'll still check it daily to be sure it's getting better and not worse." She rested Bec's arm on the table, grabbed a Sharpie from her bag and started drawing on her skin.

"What are you doing?" Bec asked with curiosity.

"Marking the streaks," she explained as she worked. "Your homework will be to keep an eye on them. If they grow past these lines," she said, showing her the ones about an inch above where the streaks ended, "you need to call me immediately."

"And if they don't?" she asked while Selina took supplies from the bag.

"I'll still clean, rewrap and inspect it tomorrow."

Bec chuckled with a nod. "Noted. I didn't know flashbangs could do this kind of damage."

"A stun grenade can do so much more than this," Selina said, inspecting the blisters with a trained eye. "They can kill in the right instances. They can also cause lasting hearing loss and tinnitus. Do you have any problems with your hearing or vision?"

"No, not since yesterday," she said, yelping when Selina sprayed something across her skin. "Could you have warned me?"

"I try not to," she answered honestly. "See, I'm used to working with a bunch of guys, and when you tell them what you're going to do, they try to get up and walk out. I've learned to ask for forgiveness after the fact." She winked, which made Bec smile. "In fairness, that was numbing spray. You'll appreciate it when I start cleaning it. Let me know when it feels tingly, and then I'll do a second layer."

"I didn't know the cleaning would be this extensive."

"I didn't know the infection was already this bad or the burn this deep. If we were in any other situation, I'd send you to the ER, but that's not an option. It's not that I can't handle this—I can, so don't worry. I just meant that they could give you intravenous antibiotics there where I can't here."

"I'm not worried," Bec said with a nod. "Something tells me even in this situation, if it were life or death, you'd be shipping me out of here."

"You'd be correct," Selina said with a lip tilt. "We aren't there yet, so I'm glad Iris mentioned it. Is it numb?" Bec nodded, so she sprayed it down again.

"She saw it last night and made me wrap it back up again. She was worried about infection."

"Guess she has some psychic abilities," Selina said with a wink as she cleaned the blessedly numb skin.

"Iris has a lot of abilities, even if her confidence in them is occasionally lacking," Bec answered, closing her eyes to avoid watching what she was doing. She was getting nauseated thinking about how badly it would hurt if it weren't mostly numb. She could feel enough to tell her it would be excruciating.

"We all care about Iris. None of us want to see her get hurt," Selina said as she ran something cool and soothing across the skin.

Bec's eyes popped open to see her swiping on burn cream. "I don't want to see her get hurt, either. If I could go in there and destroy all those pathogens, I would."

"Wasn't talking about the pathogens," Selina said, resting the arm on her elbow so she could start wrapping it in gauze.

"Oh, do you mean me? Why would I hurt Iris?"

"I'm not saying you would."

Bec bit back the eye roll since the woman held her

sore arm in her hands. “It sort of sounds like you are to my ears. Maybe you think something is going on here that isn’t?”

“Is that it?”

“Can I ask you a question?” Bec asked, hoping to buy herself time. Selina nodded, so she plastered on a smile. “Does Cal have a training school on how to answer a question with a question?”

Selina snorted with laughter, which was the response Bec was looking for. Crisis diverted. “Before I worked for Cal, I was a Chicago cop and trained search and rescue K-9 handler.”

“Which means you’re saying without saying that you’ve seen a lot of different ways someone can die?” Her lip tilt at the end was quirky in hopes Selina would laugh.

She didn’t.

“In less than fifteen seconds, I saw what I needed to see, Dr. Roth,” Selina answered, taping the wrapped gauze in place.

“It’s Bec, and I’m not sure I follow.”

“Iris trusts you, but she doesn’t trust very many people in this world. The fact that you gained her trust in less than twenty-four hours says more than words.”

“Call it forced proximity and shared terror?” Bec asked, this time dead serious.

“You could. I prefer to call it understanding and acceptance.”

“I know about lack of understanding and acceptance, so I extend it to everyone until they show me they don’t deserve it. I doubt that will ever be the case with Iris.”

Selina was silent as she packed the supplies and pulled

out bottles and vials. “Iris has suffered a lot of terrible things in life, and her family was the cause of them. She has a new family, but we won’t let anyone hurt her.”

“I’m confused about why we’re having the family exerting dominance on the new love interest discussion.”

“Offering fair warning,” Selina said. “Nothing more.”

It was Bec’s turn to snort. “You’re implying that Iris is also gay, and if I had thoughts about, what? Getting involved with her or leading her on? That I shouldn’t.”

“So you know,” Selina answered.

“It was inferred when her laptop sticker said, ‘I might look straight, but lesbihonest.’”

A smile split across Selina’s face. “She loves that sticker.” Selina drew something from a vial into a syringe.

“You’re implying that I also need one of those stickers.”

“I am implying, but lesbihonest.”

Bec’s laughter filled the room at that answer until they were both giggling. “Well played.”

Selina held up the syringe. “This is an antibiotic. Since I can’t do it intravenously, I’m going to give you a heavy bolus intramuscular and then have you take oral pills. Tomorrow, I’ll give you another bolus if we’re still in this predicament. Once I see that the oral antibiotics are clearing the lymphangitis, we can stick with them. Make sense?”

“Yep,” she said, turning in her seat so Selina could access her arm easily. “I appreciate all your help with this, Selina. The pain was getting worse by the hour.”

“I’d give you an injection of pain meds as well, but we need you alert and oriented.”

"Agreed. I can tough it out."

"Lucky for you, I have a heavy dose of ibuprofen that I'll also leave with you. Just make sure to eat something with it. But then you told me when I got down here that you planned to make Iris breakfast, right?"

With a heavy sigh, Bec shook her head. "Selina, I have no intention of hurting Iris. We're in a sticky situation here, but my only goal is to keep her calm while she tries to solve this."

"Mmm," Selina answered as she dropped the syringe into a small sharps container and tucked it in her bag. "I concur that's what I witnessed up there as you helped calm her for the sake of the facility."

"Selina—"

She held up her hand to stop her. "Listen, I'm not saying we have any control over consenting adults. I'm just saying we know how to get justice when someone we love is wronged. I'm sure you've been introduced to Iris's disabilities and understand them."

"To a degree," Bec agreed. "Her right eye has tracking issues, and the bilateral foot drop requires technologically advanced foot orthoses and an altered gait. She's been open about her neurological changes after the TBI. I've worked with a lot of neurodivergent people. I can understand the disabilities without needing to know the cause."

"Good," Selina said with a nod. "Because Iris doesn't talk about what happened to her. It's an unspoken rule that no one asks."

"And I never would," Bec agreed. "Are we done with the third degree? I should make her breakfast and keep her fueled and hydrated as she works."

Selina pushed two bottles toward her. "You've been a good sport, so yes, we're done. Take one of these three times a day," she said, pointing at the antibiotic bottle. "And one of the ibuprofen every six hours as needed. Call me if those streaks start creeping toward the line, or the arm suddenly becomes extremely hot, red and sore, or you develop a fever despite taking ibuprofen. Make sure to wrap your arm in plastic before showering. Understood?"

"You got it," Bec agreed. "Thanks again for your help. I needed it with my arm. Not so much for Iris, but I respect your position."

"I can't ask for more than that," Selina said, hoisting her bag over her shoulder. "I'll let you start cooking while I take the walkie-talkie up to Iris and check in with her."

"Great. Let her know I'll be up shortly."

"See you tomorrow," Selina said on her way out the door.

"God willing," Bec answered, to which she got a tip of Selina's fake hat.

Bec grabbed the bottles off the table and walked to the kitchenette. All she wanted to do was crawl back into bed and elevate her arm, but that wouldn't get the job done. Instead, she strapped on an ice pack over her shirt sleeve and got to work scrambling some eggs while the bread was in the toaster. She could picture Iris upstairs typing away in her own little world, but she didn't want her to do it hungry. A glance at the clock told her they were going on lunchtime instead of breakfast, but fuel was fuel, no matter the time of day.

Having the ventilation system working again was a big win for them. It wasn't as huge as the containment system, but at least the air exchanges and safety features worked again. Once Iris got the containment system online, Bec would insist she take another nap. She had no idea how long Iris had slept, but something told her it wasn't long. She got at least an hour because that's how long Bec had been awake watching Iris sleep.

Bec chuckled to herself as she buttered the toast. It sounded creepy, but it didn't feel that way last night. Iris intrigued her. Especially when she saw how peacefully she slept. It was the first time her face relaxed, and she sighed deeply. Maybe they weren't sighs of relief, but she was content. She just wanted to offer Iris contentment as much as possible while under this roof. It was easy to see that she found life difficult to navigate sometimes and that changing her daily routine was stressful for her, so if she could offer her a moment of pleasure in the day, she'd do it.

But not the kind of pleasure Selina was hinting at.

She scooped the eggs onto plates, added the toast, grabbed two bottles of orange juice from the fridge, and set it all on a tray.

She sighed heavily as she shut down the lights and rode the elevator to the main floor. It wasn't that she didn't want to offer Iris the kind of pleasure Selina implied—just the opposite was true. But working here meant putting aside her wants and desires for the betterment of humanity. Every time she stared into Iris's eyes if only for a split second, she understood the old saying, "wrong place, wrong time," all the way to her soul.

Chapter Ten

It turned out that Bec was a good cook. It was just bacon and eggs, but as far as Iris was concerned, it was exactly what she needed. She'd shoveled it in quickly so she could return to her work, which wasn't unusual. What was unusual was how she didn't want to. She wanted to linger over breakfast with a beautiful woman and enjoy her company. Had they been in any other situation, she may have, but lives were on the line, and she couldn't—wouldn't—put her team's lives at risk for her desires. Maybe once she got the containment system working again so Bec had control, she could take a rest, but not before then. Since they still hadn't heard from Ace, she could only hope he didn't realize that she'd broken his code and got part of the system back.

"No," Bec said from behind her. "No, no, no. Don't do that. No."

Iris spun around in the chair immediately. "What's the matter?" Bec pointed at the screen on her computer, which had gone blank.

"Did he just brick it?"

Iris walked over to her desk, unconsciously inhaling deeply when she got within range of the woman sitting there. Bec's body wash smelled of flowers and sunshine, bringing fond memories of her childhood. At least her childhood before her accident. She was seven when she'd been injured and rarely had memories of anything before that time. The scent reminded her of being at a park with her mother. They were laughing as they sat on a swing together. Whether it was a real memory or one fabricated by the injury was a question she'd have to ask herself later.

"Did you touch it?" Iris asked, leaning on the desk as she stared at the screen.

"No. The screen blinked, which caught my attention, and then went black. Did the cord get knocked—"

A cursor flashed on the screen, and a message started to scroll across as though someone was typing.

"'If you want to protect the world and see your colleague alive, you'll have fifty million dollars ready in forty-eight hours,'" Iris read. "'More instructions to follow. Try anything funny with the police, and you and half the world will be dead.'"

They waited silently, but nothing more came across the screen.

"We knew it was coming, but fifty million is a lot of money," Bec said as Iris texted the team. "Why cash? Why not cryptocurrency?"

"Cash is harder to trace," Iris answered, pulling Bec's chair back. When Bec looked at her in confusion, she pointed at the computer. "I don't want you to touch something and have it disappear." She opened her phone camera and took a picture of the screen. "Every cryptocurrency transaction is recorded. Especially one the size of fifty million."

"There must be a way to put tracers in the cash, right? Isn't that how they catch people all the time?"

Iris snorted, finding a little levity in the situation. "I'm certain that was the point of the 'try anything funny' line that he added. Besides, it's harder than you may think to trace the cash. They'll move it to a new bag, remove any wrappers and immediately convert it to gold bars or other untraceable currency."

"Secure One, Charlie!" Cal called as the stairwell door burst open, and he, Declan and Zac ran in.

Surprised, Iris jumped, juggling her phone as it flew up into the air until Bec grabbed it and put her arm around her waist to calm her. "Deep breath. You're safe."

Iris nodded as the team gathered around the computer to read the message.

"Doesn't seem like he knows you already have the vents back," Cal said after he read it. "We need to keep it that way."

"Agreed," Bec said. "My question is, how will he know that we will do it? We can't respond."

Iris glanced back at the computer and then held up her finger. "The cursor is still blinking. Let's see if we can reply."

She put her hands on the keyboard, but Bec's warm fingers wrapped around her wrist to stop her. "What if that bricks the computer?"

"That's a risk we have to take," Cal said from behind them. "Do you have a backup of your research?"

"Of course," Bec agreed. "But the cost to replace these machines will be astronomical for our investors."

"Not as astronomical as the cost of another global pandemic," Zac pointed out. "I'm sure they are well insured."

Bec tipped her head in agreement and motioned for her to type. Iris took a deep breath and hit the U key, but nothing happened. She felt everyone's hopes deflate, knowing they couldn't communicate with the kidnapper. Getting fifty million dollars together in two days would be extremely difficult.

"Fantastic," Bec moaned. "I've got to call the board. If I can find their contact information."

"You don't know how to reach them?" Cal asked, and Bec shook her head.

"That information was need to know, and I didn't need to know. Walter took care of the administration side of things. I could find the contact information easily if I could access his computer, but I can't."

"Do the investors have fifty million dollars?" Zac asked.

"I have no idea. I know some of their names, but I haven't been here long enough even to have met them. Again, I'd need Walter's computer, which I don't have access to."

"Yet," Iris said. "If I work all night, I might be able to break the code."

"You can't work all night," Cal said.

"But we only have forty-eight hours!" Iris exclaimed. "Do you think I can sleep knowing this virus could slip through our fingers?"

Bec lowered her hand onto Iris's shoulder, giving her a place to focus her mind other than on the anxiety. "We won't let that happen," she said. "All we need is access to the containment room. I can protect the world if you can get me inside there."

"But you can't save Walter if you don't pay them," Iris said. Cal sighed heavily, and she glanced at him. "What?"

"I think we all know that even if we pay them the money, they won't let Walter go, right?"

"Doubtful," Zac agreed.

Iris slid her hand up to her shoulder to squeeze Bec's hand. "We have to try."

"We haven't gotten proof of life," Bec said matter-of-factly. "Chances are, he's already dead, but on the off chance he's not, we have to try."

"Then we try," Cal said. "All I need is one name for an investor, and Mina will dive in and find the information. Once we have that, we'll get back together. In the meantime, Iris, you know what to do."

"I'm on it," she said, returning to her computer. "And I'm close."

"How close?" Cal asked on his way to the stairs.

"An hour. Two at the most," she said. "I'll keep you posted, but please don't come running in here like Rambo. You shave ten years off my life every time you do that."

Cal's laughter was loud as it bounced around the cavernous space. "I make no promises, but I'll try. While you're working on that, I'm heading to the motel to fill in Mina and the team at Secure Watch. Charlie, out."

Once the door to the stairwell closed, Iris turned and walked to Bec, who was standing in the same place. Without hesitating, she put her arms around her for a hug. When Bec slid her arms around Iris's waist, holding tightly to her as she buried her forehead in her shoulder, Iris felt a settling in her soul she hadn't felt with anyone ever before. For just a split second, she could be herself and offer comfort without being judged.

"We'll figure this out," Iris promised the woman in her arms. "You're not alone."

"I can't tell you how grateful I am that you're here, Iris. It's awful to feel so useless."

"I know it's hard to feel like you can't help, but you can." Iris leaned out of the hug and sat at her desk. "While I'm working on this, you can make a list of the investors' names to send to Mina. Even if you have one name, she can start tracking them down." She paused and tipped her head. "Do you think he'd have that information in one of the file cabinets?"

Bec's lips jumped into a small smile. "He might! I'll check it out while you keep working on the code."

"Mina said I need to record it whenever we mess with Walter's office."

Bec tipped her head back and forth a couple of times. "Really, what's the point now? Walter is being held for ransom, which we can prove. Recording our movements in his office proves nothing. Unless we put a camera on it that runs all day, the police can say we messed with the office when we weren't recording."

"The interior of the building isn't under surveillance?"

"Not like the outside," she said. "There was no need to record the labs all day. We go long days without messing with anything besides computers and research. If I work in a lab or with a pathogen, I turn on the cameras, which are only set up in the labs. At this point, it's worth the risk to tear apart his office and not worry about what the police will think. If we don't get the name of someone on the board, we're dead in the water. No pun intended.

I can't be certain I have the correct name, so if I give it to Mina, she could chase her tail trying to track it down."

Iris thought it over and finally nodded. "You're right. We're out of time now that Ace contacted us. See what you can find while I code."

Bec clapped once and squeezed Iris's shoulder before she took off for Walter's office. Iris turned her attention back to the computer and kept typing, her fingers working in tandem with her brain as she inserted bits and pieces of the code she used for the ventilation system. She was tired, and that made it difficult to convince her eye to keep tracking the code. Her diplopia was severe in her right eye, and even with the prism lens, when she got tired, the eye often refused to cooperate. As much as she hated to admit it, Bec and Cal were right. She'd need to sleep once she finished this—if she finished this.

Not finishing it wasn't a choice, though. She had to complete this code to protect everyone from certain death. Walter may well be dead already—there was no denying that. But if she could protect the rest of the world, then maybe he wouldn't die in vain. She could continue to hope and pray that everyone survived this, and that Ace held to his promise of releasing Walter once they had the money—if they got it. Her huff was loud in the quiet room. She had to stop this and concentrate on the task before her. If only it was that easy when, at the very least, she was trying to keep one man alive and, at the worst, the entire world. No pressure, right?

Iris could hear Bec in the office moving stuff around, crunching through glass, and opening and closing cabinets. She forced herself to concentrate on the computer screen and not turn to see what the bright beauty was doing. She'd rather spend a quiet Saturday evening with her, walking the grounds of Secure Inc., where they could sip wine as the sun set over the man-made pond at the back of the property.

"When this is over, do you want to watch the sunset with me at Secure Inc.?" she called out to Bec without turning.

"There's nothing I'd love more," Bec replied, her voice soft enough for Iris to know she was still in the office.

With a smile, she pictured them sitting on the bench on the dock, the water lapping gently against the shore as the stars came alive in the dark Minnesota sky. The dark used to scare her, but when she moved to Secure Inc., she learned to appreciate those moments of solitude when the stars were so bright that you could count them one by one. Maybe she felt safe because the property borders were so heavily guarded, or maybe she felt safe because the people within those borders were kind and understanding. It could be some of both, but over the last few years, Iris had seen a downtick in her anxiety, which made it easier for her to work with others. She still liked to work at night when fewer people crowded the space, but socializing had become more manageable, and working with the team instead of beside the team was now possible.

Something flashed in her peripheral vision, and she looked up. "Bec, what does a green light over the lab door mean?"

"That means the containment system is on," she called from the office right before footsteps ran toward her. "Is there a green light?"

"That's why I asked," Iris said, trying to keep her heart rate even as she continued to type.

"You did it! My goodness, Iris, you did it!" Bec exclaimed as she tipped her head up to stare at the light.

"Not yet," Iris answered, still typing. "The light might be on, but if I don't protect my code, he could break through it again. I don't know how closely he's paying attention to what's going on here."

Bec picked up the walkie-talkie and pressed the button. "Secure Watch, Bec," she said, releasing the button as Iris smiled. She was proud of her for remembering to follow the protocol.

"Secure One, Zulu." The box squawked with Zac's voice before Bec pushed the button down.

"Iris has the containment system active again!"

When Bec released the button, Iris heard Zac let out a whoop. "That's great news!"

Bec pushed the button, but this time, Iris jumped in. "It's good news," she clarified. "It won't be great news until I protect the code. I'm working on that now."

"Keep us posted, but it's still a great job, Iris. The elephant on my chest just lumbered off into the woods."

Iris smiled, knowing he was joking but also understanding what he meant by that. Breathing was a bit easier now that Ace didn't hold the fate of the world in his hands.

Bec set the walkie-talkie down and lowered herself to the chair. "If Ace isn't working with anyone, chances are he's busy trying to keep all the balls in the air," she said. "I would guess he also thinks his code is unbreakable."

"I was thinking about that," Iris agreed, finishing her code and hitting Enter before she spun her chair to stare at the little green light above the lab door. She did a fist pump when it stayed green and spun back to Bec. "We will have to run only the necessary functions of this place through Secure Watch computers."

"Why?" Bec asked, her head tipped.

"If I break the code entirely and it removes the malware from the computers in the facility, he will know we have control again. As long as those computers remain locked, he might well think he still controls everything and won't bother messing with anything. We only need to hold out until we have the ransom. If we don't have the money by the deadline, we'll have to make a new plan."

"I hadn't thought of that, but you're right. It's unfortunate since having access to Walter's computer would be helpful, but we'll make do."

"Did you find any of the names we can give Mina?"

Bec snapped her finger and jogged back to the office. When she returned, she held up a slip of paper. "I have several names of board members. They could also be investors. There's no way to know."

"There is one way to know," Iris assured her, grabbing her tablet as she winked. "We give those names to Mina Jacobs."

Chapter Eleven

"How is your arm?" Iris asked after they'd climbed into bed. Bec had cooked them a simple meal of frozen lasagna and garlic bread, but it had hit the spot. After checking in with Secure Watch and giving Mina the names she'd gathered from Walter's office, she had promised Mina to make Iris sleep for at least three hours before she was allowed back at the computer. Now that the containment system was working, she'd like to gain access to the labs again, but if they couldn't, at least the containment system would hold Ignis safely until she could.

"It's feeling better already," she promised the woman beside her in the dark. "I'm not just saying that, either. You were right about it getting infected, so I'm glad Selina showed up today."

Iris turned on her side to take the arm and check it over. "Me, too. Are you sure it doesn't hurt?"

"Positive," Bec promised, putting her hand over hers to stop it from fussing with the gauze. "Selina's cream and medications did the trick. It's funny, though. When I lived in the Amish community, my parents raised us around fires our entire childhood, and I never once got burned."

"You're Amish?"

Bec almost laughed until she remembered that Iris wouldn't understand that she was laughing at her tone of voice and not her question. "Not anymore," she clarified. "I left when I was sixteen."

"Left? Like you can stop being Amish?"

"You can," Bec said as Iris twined her fingers into hers. She suspected Iris didn't realize she had done it, so she made sure not to move. "It's frowned upon, of course, but when you turn sixteen, you're allowed to experience the outside world without conforming to the religion or principles."

"Rumsprouta. That's not right," she said, shaking her head.

"Close, though," Bec said. "*Rumspringa*. I had been preparing for it since I was twelve and realized that I was gay."

"I noticed the magnet," Iris said. "I'm a member, too."

"I saw the sticker on your laptop."

"Lesbihonest, I didn't need the magnet on your fridge, and you probably didn't need the sticker on my laptop," Iris said, snickering.

"Nope," she agreed.

"I assume you can't be gay and Amish?"

"Well, you can be, but you can't be out of the closet, which means you're miserable your entire life and then you die."

"Jeez, that's depressing. I may apologize for being a lot of things, but gay isn't one of them. I'm sorry they made you feel that way."

Bec smiled, squeezing her hand in agreement. "Thank you. It wasn't easy, but I knew I couldn't live that way. On the first day of my *Rumspringa*, I went to the public library and read about science and how it affects our world. We weren't taught much science in school, but what little they did teach us intrigued me, and I wanted to know more. We were taught that being gay was a sin and something that only happened in other cultures, but science taught me that being gay is part of human nature and not just certain cultures. I could never go back after learning the truth and feeling so deceived by my parents. At that same library the next day, I saw a poster on their announcement board. It was an open-door support group for gays and lesbians, and as I'm naturally curious, I decided to go. Truthfully, I didn't know what I was looking for when I walked through the doors, but by the time I left, I knew what I'd found. An entire community of people who lived full lives in loving relationships who promised they would help me survive outside my family."

"That's how you became a scientist?"

"To make a long story short, yes. Several couples let me live with them so I could go to high school and then college. They helped me get everything I didn't have to survive in the world, like a social security number, vaccines and a job. I was lucky. There are a lot of kids who can't escape their religion or family to be their authentic selves. I try to help as much as possible with Out to Innovate. They do so much for LGBTQ+ youth."

"I knew you were smart, strong and brave, but I didn't know how much until you shared that with me. Thank you."

Bec turned on her side and slipped her hand up Iris's cheek, stroking her temple with her thumb. Connecting with her when she wasn't wearing her glasses was nice.

She felt like she could see her beautiful soul for the first time. "I hope you understand I didn't want to leave my family."

"Of course, you didn't. You wanted them to accept you for who you are, which wasn't too much to ask. When they didn't, you made the only choice you could. Look what you've done with your life since making that excruciating decision. I'm proud of you, Bec. I know it wasn't easy."

"I really want to kiss you right now," she whispered, her thumb straying to Iris's lips to rub across them.

"I wouldn't object."

Before Iris could finish the thought, Bec took her lips. They were soft, warm and tasted of the sweet wine they'd had with dinner. Just a little, she'd said as Bec poured, insisting they had to be clearheaded for work. She was the furthest thing from clearheaded with Iris's lips on hers, but she didn't care. She'd been dreaming about kissing Iris since she'd walked into her lab no more than a day ago. Bec had never believed people when they said, "When you know, you know," but how wrong she'd been. The sweet way Iris sighed when Bec slipped her tongue along the edge of her lips told her she sensed it, too.

"You are the most unexpected part of this whole situation, Iris Knowles," she said, kissing her way to the woman's neck to rest her lips against her pulse. It was fast from their kiss, but it slowed the longer she caressed Iris's collarbone with her thumb and tenderly kissed her skin.

"When I saw you on the screen, my heart slowed, and my anxiety disappeared for the first time in as long as I can remember. I didn't know why, but I knew I'd do anything to help you. I wondered if you were who I'd been looking for in life, but I struggled to believe that was possible—until we met. The way you understood, accepted and didn't judge me made you the first in my life ever to do that."

"That makes me sad, Iris," Bec whispered, stroking her chest as she spoke. "We're all different, but in the end, we're all the same. We want to give love and be loved. That's all any human wants."

Iris slipped her hand under Bec's shirt, cupping her rib cage with a silent question in her eyes. When Bec nodded, their lips connected, and so did their hearts.

IRIS FORCED HER concentration back on the screen as she tried to write a malware patch for the lab doors. It wasn't as imperative to have access to the labs now that they had the containment system working, but she would do what she could while the rest of the team tried to track down the money to use for ransom. The last update she'd gotten from Cal was Mina had found one board member, Allen McCarthy of California. He was currently out of the country, but they were conferring with him to explain why it was so important that the police weren't called until after Walter was returned safely. She still expected Bec to hear about this debacle from him or one of the other board members he was likely to contact.

Bec.

Her fingers strayed to her lips briefly before she forced them back to the keyboard. After knowing her barely twenty-four hours, she'd made love to the gorgeous scientist. That was so not her MO. Intimacy was usually tricky for her, but it wasn't with Bec. Natural. Unhurried. Romantic. Intimate. Those were all words she could use to describe making love to Bec. She was gentle, understanding, patient and loving. They had passed out in a tangle of limbs afterward, and when Iris woke about an hour ago, she hated to leave her. Unfortunately, duty called, so she slipped from the bed without disturbing her.

The story Bec had told her about leaving her community and depending on others in an entirely new one kept running through her mind. She had to have so much bravery and strength at such a young age to do something so drastic, yet she'd come out the other side a successful scientist. Everyone told Iris she was brave for what she'd gone through in life, but she didn't have a choice. Bec did, which made her so much braver for taking the step to go it alone.

Something caught her eye, and she stopped long enough to write it down. Then she started again, surprised when she saw the same thing a few lines later. Her heart rate picked up as she grabbed her tablet, took a shot of the computer screen and typed out a message to Mina before sending it. If what she was seeing in the code was a signature, Mina would know faster than anyone. In the meantime, she'd keep going, channeling the feel under her fingers of the labs clicking open as they unlocked, allowing them entrance. She vowed to stop short of unlocking them, though. She wanted Bec to be awake and ready to enter the lab to ensure all pathogens were safely tucked away. The last thing she wanted was to have those doors slide open and something to spill out.

A shudder went through her, so she dropped her hands from the keyboard and walked to the restroom at the end of the hall. Once done, she stopped in the break room for a coffee from the Keurig and a pastry that Cal had sent over from home base. She was grateful he kept the room stocked for them since the Secure One team had set up their break room in the basement, so they didn't have to announce themselves whenever they wanted coffee. She had to admit it was easier on her nerves.

When she returned to her desk, her phone rang, so she grabbed it and swiped it open. "Secure Watch, India."

"Secure Watch, Whiskey. I got your code."

"Oh, good," Iris said, spinning in her chair to stare at the screen again. "I'm hoping that's Ace's signature."

"It could be, but I need more than this. I'm going to remote access your laptop, so save your work. I didn't want to screw anything up."

"You're good to go," she promised after hitting several keys. "Did you sort out the situation with the board?"

"We're in the process. I'm convinced he understands the importance of the situation now, so once he contacts the rest of the board, we'll work with them to get the money. It will be tight to get that much money so quickly."

"You don't think Walter is still alive, do you?" Iris asked, noting the tone of her voice. She was resigned, a surefire bet that Mina felt it was all in vain.

"I don't know what to think," she admitted, and Iris could hear her keyboard clicking on the line. "This was planned in a way that says whoever is behind it has a serious grudge against the facility or someone in it, but all of the previous scientists and employees check out."

"At least the ones you can look into," Iris pointed out. "We can't access all of the files, making it harder to get the full picture."

"That's true, but I've been fortunate to reach out to some of the past scientists who gave me names of other employees they worked with at the time. I know it's not a comprehensive list, but with our limitations, it's better than nothing."

"Did you talk to any of those new names?" Iris asked.

"I spoke with two of the scientists. When I asked why they left, they reiterated the same thing Bec had. Walter was difficult to work with as a colleague. He disliked working long hours and spent more time at home than in the facility. They didn't want to say more, but the overall vibe was that management was a problem."

"I wonder why the board kept Walter on as their administrator when people were in and out like a revolving door."

"I can't say for certain, but I would bet none of them reported Walter's inability to manage to be their reason for leaving. That would only reflect poorly on them in the industry, and let's face it, everyone knows everyone in that community. Not to mention, I can't imagine it would be easy to find well-qualified individuals who want to live isolated for years on end. If the—"

Mina paused and fell silent, but Iris knew her boss well enough not to hang up until she told her to. Either she was hot on the trail, or she would have more questions for her. Her mind returned to the woman downstairs, wondering if things would be awkward in the light of day. Something told her it wouldn't be. What they had shared was pure, open and honest, and when you share open communication, there's nothing left to feel awkward about.

"What?" Mina asked, and Iris snapped to attention.

"I didn't say anything."

"I know. I'm asking what because the source code control system tells me this malware was written on a computer connected to the service inside the facility."

"That's not possible, Mina. There has to be a mistake," Iris said, leaning forward to peer at her screen as though it held all the answers.

"There has to be. Give me ten, and I'll call you back."

The line went dead. Iris held the phone as the back of her neck prickled. Unless it wasn't impossible. Maybe the person who wrote the code was sleeping off their lovemaking just below her feet.

Chapter Twelve

Bec woke slowly, confused and disoriented by the bright light that had her squinting against it. She was on her stomach, her arms behind her back as someone tried to tie her wrists together.

"Help!" she screamed, unsure if the Secure One team could hear her from where they were. "Somebody help me!" She kicked and fought, finally getting the better of the person so she could flip over. Her lips froze on the next call for help when Iris was the person holding a computer cord in her hands with her eyes wild. "Iris, what are you doing?"

"I'm stopping you from hurting anyone!" she exclaimed, her eyes darting around the room. "I trusted you!"

Bec raised her hands in front of her and tried to speak calmly. "Iris, I don't know what you're talking about. Why would I hurt someone?"

Iris reeled off a bunch of numbers and letters that only confused her more. "Does that ring a bell?"

"No, Iris. I don't know what you're talking about. What is going on?"

"We know, Dr. Roth," she said, and Bec's gut sank when she used her full name.

"Know what, Iris?"

"That the malware was written on a computer attached to the mainframe within the facility."

Bec stood but kept her hands out in front of her to show she wasn't being aggressive. She wanted to calm Iris down but not scare her. "I don't know what a mainframe is. Is that a computer?"

"Everyone knows what a mainframe is!" Iris exclaimed and Bec shook her head slowly.

"I've heard the term, but I don't do computers for a living. What was that other thing you said? All the numbers and letters."

"That was a line of code from the malware I'm trying to patch. Mina said it originated here."

"If that's true," Bec said softly in hopes she'd listen to her, "It didn't come from me. I don't know how to write code. I can perform the tasks I need to, but they don't include that. If that were required for the job, I'd have to attend code-writing school."

Iris snorted as she rolled her eyes. "Code-writing school. It's called computer science. You must have taken that in college."

"I took computer classes, sure, but never for coding," Bec promised. "There are specific programs we use here for different aspects of the research, but none of them were written here. They're available nationwide to any lab who purchases a license."

Iris dropped the cord to her side and took a step toward her. "What's Python?"

"A snake?"

"Java? PHP?" Iris asked and Bec grasped the other woman's elbows.

"Coffee and a drug? No, that's PCP. What's PHP?"

"Python, Java and PHP are all types of coding languages. Java has been around forever, Bec."

"I grew up isolated from electricity, much less computers," Bec reminded her. "By the time I started public school, I was so far behind that the only way to graduate was to concentrate on the core classes. It wasn't me, Iris. Why would I call you in to help me secure the labs if I was the one who wrote the malware? That doesn't make sense."

"But you said Walter doesn't know anything about computers, either."

"He always acted like he didn't," Bec confirmed.

"Who takes care of your technology needs then?" Iris asked as Bec pulled on clothes.

"An IT firm, as far as I know. That information should be in Walter's files. Let's go look."

Iris waited while Bec used the bathroom and brushed her teeth, which gave her a few minutes to calm her breathing and try not to be hurt that Iris thought she was capable of this kind of deception. Once she got Iris to calm down, she could see in her eyes that she was scared and confused, but Iris didn't really believe she had anything to do with writing the code.

"How did you figure out the code was written in the facility?" she called from where she put her socks and shoes on.

"I found a suspicious line of code and sent it to Mina."

She grabbed her phone, slipping it into her pocket just in case one of the investors called her. "You said you were going to look for a signature. Is that what you meant?" she asked as they hurried upstairs. Bec would have preferred to start the day with a kiss and a cup of coffee instead of accusations and attempted confinement, but this was not a normal day.

“I’m sorry for trying to tie you up and making accusations that weren’t true,” Iris said as they stood in the elevator. “I shouldn’t have let the anxiety take over the way it did. You’ve been here the whole time helping me, so I should have known you weren’t behind it because that doesn’t even make sense, but—”

Bec put her finger to Iris’s lips before she hit the stop button on the elevator panel. “But you are under a lot of stress, and fighting the anxiety is hard minute to minute in a situation like this. Suddenly discovering that the code was written in the facility made it easy to jump to conclusions.”

“Yes, but I shouldn’t have. Not after last night. I know you on a level that…”

She paused and Bec waited, but she didn’t finish the thought. She slipped her arms around Iris’s waist and snugged them belly to belly. “You know me on a soul-deep level that strips away everything but the truth, even if we’ve only known each other for a few days?”

“Yes,” Iris whispered, lowering her forehead to touch hers. “You said I can’t say I’m sorry, but I truly am.”

“I’m not upset, sweetheart,” she promised, lifting her face to kiss her lips. “I understand that you’re stressed and tired, not to mention scared. We can get through this if we trust each other, okay?”

Iris didn’t answer with words. She lowered her head and kissed Bec deeply, reminding Bec of the passion and desire they had shared last night when they bared their souls to each other. Bec smiled at the woman when the kiss ended, gazing deeply into her eyes. Her heart melted, knowing she trusted her enough to do that without fear.

"What do you say we get to the bottom of this nightmare so we can get on with living?" When Iris nodded, Bec hit the start button for the elevator.

"I find it difficult to believe that an IT firm would be behind this," Iris said as they left the elevator and walked toward Walter's office.

"Unless it's one bad apple that they don't know is in their midst," Bec answered, skirting the glass still on the floor as they walked into the office. "I sure wish we had access to the security videos."

Iris leaned on the desk and crossed her arms over her chest. "Why? There's no way to know when the code was written, so it's a needle in a haystack situation."

"No, not for the coder," Bec said, pulling out the drawer marked operations and rifling through the files. "For the kidnapper. Something is bugging me about the person, but I can't put my finger on it. The flash-bang disoriented me and blurred my vision, but I feel like they were familiar."

Iris pushed herself up and grabbed the walkie-talkie off her belt. "Secure Watch, India."

"Secure One, Charlie."

"Cal? Are you here?"

"Just arrived with Selina," he answered when she released the button.

"Would you come to the lab? We have a question."

"Ten-four."

"Oh great, he brought the torture nurse with him," Bec muttered with a grimace.

Iris immediately pulled her into her arms. "She means

well and is trying to keep you from getting worse. I'll hold your hand if that will help."

Bec patted her back before ending the hug. "That was a joke, Iris. I very much appreciate Selina. I was teasing."

"Oh. Sorry, I'm not good at picking out sarcasm or teasing. I take things quite literally."

"No need to apologize. I should have thought of that. I'll tell you the next time I'm teasing, okay?" Iris nodded as Bec returned to the cabinet to pull out the file she'd been looking for, holding it up in victory. "Got it!"

"Let's go to the lab and wait for Cal," Iris said, motioning for Bec to go first. They were barely out of the office when Iris's tablet started ringing. She grabbed it from the desk and hit the answer button. "Secure Watch, Whiskey."

"Secure Watch, India," Iris said, and Mina joined them on the screen.

"Is Bec there?" Mina asked, and Iris nodded. She walked over to a high lab table and propped the tablet so she could see them both.

"Good morning, Mina."

"Hey, Bec. I know Cal and Selina are on the way, but I discovered some information about one of the employees I wanted to run past you."

"Sure, whatever I can do to help. I haven't personally worked with many of them, though."

"This one you have," Mina said. "Zafar Zimmer."

"Yes, our lab tech. He's been here as long as Dr. Hoerman, so close to six years. I've only been here five months. What about him?"

"I don't think he exists."

"What now?" Bec asked, glancing at Iris before turning back to Mina. "I work with him every day."

"What I mean is, I don't think his real name is Zafar Zimmer. The few people in the world with that name don't live in the United States, nor have they bought plane tickets to Poland from the United States."

"Maybe he used a different last name, or someone else bought the ticket for him?" Bec suggested, but Mina shook her head.

"Even if someone else bought it, the ticket must be in his name. There were no passengers on any flight to Poland over the last year with the name Zafar. There were only ten males in the age range you gave me for your lab tech who flew to Poland on or around the dates you gave me. None of them were named Zafar, and none of them were your lab tech."

"I don't understand what's going on," Bec admitted. "Should I try calling him?"

"We already did," Mina said. "We got the message the number was disconnected, changed or no longer in service."

"What is going on?" Bec asked just as the door to the stairs opened.

"Secure One, Charlie," Cal said as he walked in with Selina.

"Hi," Iris said, turning to them. "We're talking to Mina."

Mina took a moment to catch Cal and Selina up on their discussion.

"Right before she called, we were in Walter's office," Iris said. "We were looking for the file with the information for the IT company the research center uses to see if they would know who had written the code."

"Did you find it?" Cal asked. Bec nodded, tapping the file on the table.

"But in the process, Bec said she wished she could see the security footage from the day of the kidnapping."

"Why?" Selina asked. "You said the person was dressed head to toe in black."

"They were," Bec agreed. "But they seemed familiar to me. I can't explain it more than that. I caught a glimpse of them after my vision cleared from the flash-bang, but not enough to put my finger on it."

"I'm afraid there's no way to look at the camera footage," Cal said.

"We know," Iris agreed. "The footage can only be watched on Walter's computer."

"Not what I meant. The malware virus also disabled the security cameras. None of them were active when we arrived."

"That doesn't make sense," Bec said. "Those cameras don't even go down when the power goes out. They stream on Walter's computer, but he can transfer them to my computer or tablet when he leaves for the night since we're always running double duty out here."

"When I checked them on arrival, they were turned off," Cal explained. "I didn't turn them back on since there was no way to watch them with the computers not working, and it didn't matter since we were providing security. You didn't turn them off?"

"Absolutely not," Bec answered. "We don't get much traffic out here, but they alert us if someone arrives at the loading dock or approaches any of the doors."

"What about at night?" Cal asked. "Who watches them at night?"

"My apartment has a computer that I run them on there as well, and it emits an alarm if anything is amiss and wakes me."

"Why doesn't the facility have a security company to handle the cameras?" Mina asked, her head tipped to the side. "Someone that could call for outside help if anything happened to the few of you inside."

"I asked the same question," Bec said, facing Mina again. "Walter told me the company was always messing up, so the board agreed to move them in-house. I don't know when, but it's been this way since I started working here."

Mina raised a brow. "Sounds fishy to me."

"Fishier than a Friday night smelt fry at the VFW," Cal agreed. "Especially since the cameras were manually turned off."

"I meant to ask how you secured the side door again after the kidnapper broke in?" Bec asked, spinning toward Cal.

He stood there staring at her, his head tipped in confusion. "Secured the side door? It wasn't broken. You buzzed me in, which I assumed was how you always did it. The biometrics system was down, but the door was locked. Since then, we've used the loading dock to go in and out."

Bec closed her eyes and tried to fight the rising panic as her heart pounded. "Cal, if that's true, then—"

"The kidnapper had a key," Selina finished.

"Does Zafar have a key, Bec?" Mina asked.

Bec stumbled backward, caught by the warm chest

of the woman she'd spent the night with. "We—we all do," she said, fear and anger making her body and voice shake.

"Sit," Selina ordered, pressing a chair under her and helping her down before she took her pulse. "Take some deep breaths."

Bec did what she said, and the spots in front of her eyes slowly disappeared. "I'm sorry, but it struck me that only three of us have keys to this place."

"You, Zafar and Walter?" Mina asked, and Bec nodded.

"With the caveat that my vision was wonky after the flash-bang, it's entirely possible the kidnapper was Zafar."

Chapter Thirteen

Iris put her arm around Bec's shoulders, hoping it would stop her quaking. "It's okay," she whispered. "Tell us why you think that?"

"He was the same height and build," Bec said, her words shaky. "I know that doesn't mean anything since there are plenty of six-foot-tall skinny guys in the world, but not as many who know how to navigate this facility in silence or where Walter's office is."

"Did the kidnapper have to walk past you to get to Walter's office?" Cal asked, and Bec nodded immediately. Iris held her tighter, hoping to offer her strength and warmth.

"Yes, yes," Bec said, turning in the chair and pointing to the spot by the lab door. "I was there when the flash-bang went off."

"That's close to the hallway," Cal said, walking over there. "But you didn't see anyone down here?"

"No, but I had just half turned back toward Walter's office to answer a question he'd asked me. Then the bang and the light disoriented me until I caught a glimpse of the kidnapper in the office with Walter."

"Which means the kidnapping was targeted because it would have been easier to take you and run," Mina said.

"Unless it was opportunity driven," Cal said to her point. "He may have realized that she was stunned, so better to take the guy who could still move quickly and call for help."

Someone handed Mina a piece of paper off camera, and everyone was silent while she read it. When she glanced up, Iris knew the game had changed.

"Unless the good doctor was in on it." Mina waved the paper in the air.

"In on what?" Bec looked around, confused, until Mina clarified.

"A fifty-million-dollar payday."

"No." Bec shook her head. "Absolutely not. Walter wasn't hurting for money and was close to retirement."

"You're correct. He wasn't hurting for money now." Mina shook the paper in her hand. "But Walter Hoerman was deep in debt until a few years ago."

"Does it say to who?" Cal asked.

"According to this, just about everyone, including the taxman."

"What on earth?" Bec asked. "Where was all his money going?"

"Gambling?" Selina suggested.

"That's possible, though I can only see his verifiable debts."

Cal shook his head as he leaned on the lab table. "Regardless, I smell a rat or two, but they aren't in Poland."

"Same," Mina, Iris and Selina said in unison, giving them a moment of levity in a situation that was anything but funny.

"I think that Walter got in over his head with something, then took a payoff to clear his debt. Chances are, that payoff came with stipulations, and he devised a way to get out from under the thumb of his creditors. He befriends a young, impressionable kid and convinces him he'll get half of the big payday for writing some malware and fake kidnapping him."

Mina shrugged as she leaned on her desk, fatigue written on her face. "Anything is possible, but what concerns me is that Zafar is untraceable, which feels like a—"

"Setup," Selina finished. Since she'd been set up not too long ago by her thought-to-be-dead sister, she would smell a similar ploy from a mile away.

"Zafar was playing ball for two bad guys?" Iris asked, glancing at Selina. "But who?"

"That's the fifty-million-dollar question," Mina said.

"You mean the sixty-four-dollar question," Iris corrected, then she noticed Mina's raised brow. "Oh, right. Fifty-million-dollar ransom."

"The problem is, there's no way to confirm this," Bec pointed out. "We conveniently cannot access Walter's computer, and the cameras were off during the kidnapping."

"I tried tracing Zafar's phone, but the last time it pinged was a week ago. That lines up with the dates you said he'd be gone to Poland," Mina said to Bec, who nodded. "But it also says it's no longer in service, so I believe he ditched the phone rather than flying off to Poland."

Cal nodded. "Agreed."

"Did you track Walter's phone?" Iris asked.

"Walter has his phone?" Mina asked, but Bec answered.

"I believe he does. He was holding it when the kidnapper broke in, and it's nowhere to be found here."

Mina grinned, which told Iris she was pleased with this information. "I have the number. Do you know if he has the find-my-phone feature on it?"

"It was the latest model, so I'm sure it's there. I don't know if it's on. Don't you think he'd shut it off, though? Everyone knows cell phones can't be traced if they're off."

"Everyone should know that," Selina said with a snicker. "But not everyone has a Mina Jacobs on their team who can get around pesky things like powered down phones."

Mina winked. "Whiskey, out."

"That was a strange turn of events." Bec turned to look up at Iris. "I'm concerned."

"We're all concerned," Cal agreed. "But until Mina gets back to us, there isn't much we can do. Selina will take you to the apartment to check your arm while we're waiting. Then we can get together once Mina calls back."

Bec pushed herself up from the chair and patted Iris's shoulder as she walked by with Selina.

Once they were gone, Cal sighed. "I was afraid this could be an inside job."

"You were? Why?" Iris asked, surprised to hear him say that.

"Nothing quite added up. If it had been one thing, I could have written it off, but not all of this."

"What can we do in the meantime?" She stared at the floor, wishing to be with Bec, but she didn't want to look clingy or needy.

"How close are you to regaining access to the labs?"

"I don't know," she admitted. "Less than an hour is my hope. But I don't want to unlock the labs until Bec is ready to go in and be sure everything is locked down."

"And once that's done, where are we with the systems?"

"Once we can get into the labs, we'd control all the important systems, including the biometrics. I don't want to take full control back and unlock the computers in case he's paying attention to his code. If he thinks we've got control of the facility again, thereby rendering his hostage useless, then he has no reason to keep him alive."

"Unless his hostage is in on it." Cal used air quotes around *hostage*, to which she nodded. "I agree with you, though. Let's work on access to the labs while we wait for Mina. We can make a better plan once she gets back to us."

Iris checked her watch. "We have twenty-seven hours until the ransom is due, and we haven't heard from the board, either. That doesn't give us much time."

"It sure doesn't, but you do your job, and I'll do mine. Hopefully, the two will align so we can get to the bottom of this before anyone else gets hurt."

Cal patted her on the shoulder and left the room, allowing her to ponder if that was true. Leaving here—leaving Bec—was going to hurt.

"ARE YOU SURE this is okay?" Iris asked as she was nearly finished with the code to unlock the labs.

Bec knelt before her and grasped her chin, forcing eye contact with her for a second before Iris looked over her shoulder. "I'm positive, Iris. The lab is a level three lab, which means there's an airlock between the door you're going to open and the one that holds the bad guys. Only I can open the one that holds the bad guys. I'll go in, get dressed, put on my ventilator and then use my biometrics to enter the lab."

"But what about anything that escapes when you open the second door? Something bad could happen to you. That's what I'm worried about."

"Nothing can escape because of air pressure. I'll wear my safety equipment, so I'm protected even if something is floating around the lab that didn't get trapped in the filters, but I don't believe that's the case. It's a lot to explain right now, but trust me, there's no risk to me or you if you open that door."

"Can I talk to you when you're in the lab?" Iris asked, still unsure how she felt about letting her go in there alone. Not that she had any choice in the matter, but she didn't have to like it.

"Unfortunately, no. Normally, we have a comms system that allows for that, but you don't have time to get that working, so we'll use sign language. I'll give you a thumbs-up once I'm in the lab and know everything is good, okay?"

"And if it's not good?"

"I'll give you a thumbs-down, but we'll have bigger problems on our hands at that point," she said with a wink. "Do you trust me?"

"Yes, but I'm also concerned about you getting hurt."

Bec took her hands and leaned up, passionately kissing her but without lingering. "That's one thing you don't have to be concerned about. I plan to kiss you ten thousand more times, so I will follow every safety protocol and take zero risks. Okay?"

"For the first time in my life, I want to hold someone to a promise like that, Bec."

"And I want to be the first one who doesn't break one to you." Bec caressed her face before she dropped her hand and walked to the lab door. "Ready when you are, sweetheart."

With butterflies in her belly, Iris put her hands on the keyboard and finished the code before she hit Enter. The light over the door switched to red, and Bec used her credentials to open the door. She gave her a thumbs-up and blew her a kiss before the door slid closed again and locked the woman she cared about inside a room with dangerous pathogens. The thought struck her, and she stilled. She cared about Bec, and not just as a friend or colleague. She cared about her as a love interest.

The surprise was less from the idea that she could care about Bec as a love interest and more from the fact that she could care about her as a lifelong partner. Her past relationships had all ended for the same reason, at least according to what they told Iris as they broke up with her. They were convinced she couldn't care about another person deeply in a lasting relationship. They tried to break it to her in an "it's not your fault" kind of way, but over time, it ate at her until she believed that she could never love someone deeply enough for them to stay.

Now, gazing at Bec as she worked inside the lab protected by the bubbled hazmat suit, she could see she was waiting for the right woman to love deeply. Too bad the right woman was one she could never have even if she would always care about her. They were too different in both experiences and distance. Bec lived here, and even if she left the facility after this situation, she would work somewhere else at a college or university far from Secure Inc. While Iris could work remotely and remain employed by Secure Watch, she worried the stress would be too much for her, and she'd fail at the relationship and her job.

After protecting her patch for the doors, she pushed herself to standing and blew out a breath. It was time to quarantine those thoughts to the background, as they had too much to do to worry about what would happen after this case was over. If they didn't get a bead on Walter or Zafar before the end of today, she couldn't predict what would happen. They didn't have fifty million dollars, and convincing the investors to give that up for one man, when they already knew they had control of the facility again, would take more time than they had.

With one last glance at Bec, still working inside the lab, Iris walked to Walter's office. It was time to get to the bottom of this so everyone could safely move on with their lives. Well, everyone but Walter.

Chapter Fourteen

Iris stood staring at the giant cherrywood desk that occupied most of the office. The wood gleamed, clearly polished regularly by someone who cared. The top was neat and orderly, with only a blotter, pencil holder and computer monitor. There had to be information somewhere in the behemoth to tell them if Walter and Zafar were in this together. If Walter wanted out from under someone's control, this plot could be driven by desperation rather than greed. If that was the case, and Walter was behind this, why was Secure Watch on the job? She couldn't figure out why Walter had allowed Bec to call Secure Watch if he was the mastermind behind this scheme.

Her gaze drifted to the shattered glass next to Walter's office door, and Iris couldn't help but wonder if they hadn't intended to keep Bec alive long enough for it to matter. Walter wouldn't have a choice but to let Bec attempt to get help to reboot their system, but if they planned to kill her before Secure Watch arrived, then he wouldn't need to argue with her about it. He could let her make the call, knowing it wouldn't matter anyway. A shudder racked her at the thought of losing that beautiful woman who was valiantly fighting to save them all from being killed by putting herself between them and some deadly bugs.

But if that was his plan, why was she still alive? Had the gunman thought he'd hit her? According to Bec, that was possible since when the glass broke, she fell backward. Maybe they hadn't stuck around long enough to double-check, which was a mistake on their part, but one Iris was so glad they had made. She walked to his desk and faced off with it, knowing the computer was useless but wondering if he had anything in the drawers to give them a place to start. A name. A phone number. Anything that could give them a lead about where they might be.

She sat in his desk chair and started pulling open desk drawers, which, unfortunately, were ridiculously tidy. Other than office supplies, there weren't random slips of paper or business cards that didn't belong. She lifted the blotter, hoping something might be taped to the desk, but again, she was disappointed. There was no point in searching for a hidden drawer in the desk. That was a little too mystery-novelish even for her.

The thought that something might be taped to the desk ran through her mind, and she got down on her hands and knees, searching under the desk drawers for any scrap of paper taped anywhere. Nothing. Undeterred, she searched behind the filing cabinet and inside each drawer before starting on the files. She glanced over her shoulder to check on Bec, who was still working inside the lab.

Iris was determined to search every file, but ten minutes later, she was still empty-handed. He must have kept anything he didn't want found at home. That was the only answer. She would have to send Cal or one of the other team members over to his place to search. The information had to be somewhere unless he was innocent. If he was, that made this a wild-goose chase that ended in Walter dying when the ransom wasn't paid.

Iris sat on the edge of the desk to rub her face from exhaustion, fear and sadness. One way or the other, the events at the Research Center of the Advancement of Biogenics would be over soon and she would have to return to Secure Inc. with the team, leaving behind the only woman she'd ever cared about in life. That was a tough pill to swallow, made more so by the fact that regardless of how she felt about Bec, there was no way someone like her would ever want to be in a long-term relationship with a woman riddled with anxiety, fear and compulsions.

The thought stood Iris up straight. The anxiety and fear were there, but her compulsions had faded since she arrived. For the first time since the incident, she was functioning without everything being exactly how she thought she needed it. Maybe it was just the situation she was in and nothing more. Her therapist had told her years ago that a change in her routine was necessary if she was going to heal from the past and find any enjoyment in life. Iris hadn't believed her for a hot second. Her brain was wired differently now, meaning she would always deal with the consequences of that day, right?

As the anxiety medication lessened her fear about facing each day, the intensity of her compulsions slowly lessened, too. She still liked things orderly, but she could handle slightly more chaos in her routine short-term. What she was dealing with here was more than chaos, though. Her anxiety should be through the roof despite her medication, but she had found a way to remain relatively calm through it. Bec was the reason. She was sure of it. Iris searched her memory for the last time she had done her mental repeating to soothe herself. It was something she'd done since the incident to keep her anxiety lower or at bay. As a child, she was convinced that nothing bad would happen as long as she did it once every hour.

New places aren't safe. You can't trust anyone. No one can love you now.

Iris paused at the thought. *No one can love you now.* She'd been telling herself that for twenty-six years! No wonder it had become a self-fulfilling prophecy. When she glanced over her shoulder and laid eyes on Bec, she forced herself to change those inner thoughts.

Some new places aren't safe. Stay guarded. You can trust the people who have proven themselves to you. You deserve love, and your past doesn't make you unlovable.

After lowering herself to Walter's desk chair, she waited. Waited for the feelings of fear to spike and the trembling to begin. While she waited, she focused on Bec in the lab, walking back and forth between the sink and a giant hood that covered half the room. She repeated the phrase aloud this time. "Some new places aren't safe. Stay guarded. You can trust the people who have proven themselves to you. You deserve love, and your past doesn't make you unlovable."

Again, she waited. Her heart rate didn't rise beyond unacceptable levels, she didn't start to sweat, and her hands didn't tremble. She glanced down at them to see they had a slight tremor, but nothing like she was used to.

Iris said the phrases again and then again until the

words came to her as easily as the old ones used to. Was she healed? No. She was still clammy, and her heart raced, but underneath it was a peace she hadn't felt in twenty-six years. Her gaze strayed to the woman dressed like an astronaut still walking around the lab. Maybe surrounding yourself with the right people was the answer. The only way to know was to keep doing it, but that would be impossible if they didn't figure out what Walter knew. She pulled the walkie-talkie off her belt and pressed the button. "Secure Watch, India."

"Secure One, Charlie," Cal answered.

"I've been searching Walter's office for anything that might tell us what he knows or if he's behind this," she said, releasing the button.

"Did you find anything?"

"Nothing, which is also suspicious if you ask me. He has to be keeping it at home or in his car."

"We've checked his car. There was nothing."

"I think it's time we check his house. The information we need to save him might be there."

She released the button and waited for Cal to respond while keeping an eye on Bec. It looked like she was finishing up and decontaminating her suit.

"We were just talking about that," Cal agreed. "I'll put together a team and head over there. I don't have permission to enter the property, but I'll find a way in."

"That sounds good. Can you keep me posted?" she asked, releasing the button and waiting for him to respond.

"Will do. We'll gear up and head over there. Charlie, out."

Iris set the walkie-talkie down on the desk and sighed

as she pulled open a drawer. If she was sending Cal to Walter's house to look for information, she'd check the desk one more time for completeness as well. Then, if Cal also found nothing, they could say with certainty it was nowhere that they could easily access it.

If she wanted to hide something, she would put it in the biggest drawer, so she pulled it out of the desk and dumped it out, disappointed when the bottom of the drawer was solid. After cleaning up the mess, she slid it back into the desk and pulled out the middle drawer, doing the same thing and earning the same result. There was only one more drawer, so she pulled it out, but when she dumped it, something thunked. Her heart started racing as she realized despite the drawer being empty, it was far heavier than it should be. She set it on its edge on the desk and inspected the bottom panel, surprised when the bottom of the drawer was a different color than the inside top layer. There was no way to know that unless you pulled it out, which told her it was on purpose.

The question was, how did it open? She wiggled the top piece of wood, but it didn't give. There wasn't a hole to hook her finger or an indication that it should open. "Because it shouldn't," she said, flipping it over so the bottom faced up. There was a hinge halfway down the drawer and a cloth tab. She pulled the tab, and the drawer came open, revealing a laptop nestled between the two pieces of wood. It wasn't easy, but she wiggled it free of the drawer. Had she found what they were looking for?

"Iris? What is that?" Bec asked as she stepped into the room.

Iris swung toward her with the computer in her hand and grinned. "Walter's only chance."

Chapter Fifteen

"Is that Walter's computer?" Bec asked in shock as Iris joined her in the doorway.

"I found it in his desk, so I sure hope so. We're about to find out, but first, tell me everything was alright in the lab?"

"Yes," Bec said with a head nod. "Nothing escaped, and all the safety protocols worked. I've secured all the viruses, so they can't hurt anyone."

"That's a relief," Iris said as they walked to the workspace. She'd searched the drawer but couldn't find a charger, so if the computer had no juice, they'd have to wait for Cal to tear apart Walter's house before learning what secrets it held.

"I still can't believe you found a computer," Bec said, squeezing Iris's shoulder. "You may have single-handedly saved Walter's life if he's not behind this."

"Once I had the lab doors working again, it made sense to try and figure out where to look for information on how to save Walter before the deadline was up. I was hoping to find a phone number or name to give Mina so she could run a trace, but I found nothing. I wasn't even going to check the drawers. It felt too…"

"On the nose?"

Iris nodded, her lips tilting up a bit. "Exactly that, so I didn't check them the first time through. Once I convinced Cal to go to Walter's house, I decided to do my due diligence, too. It was in the top drawer, but I started at the bottom. Nearly gave up, if I'm honest."

"So glad you didn't," Bec said, leaning down and kissing her lips. She'd intended to keep the kiss light and easy, but it quickly heated and morphed into a kiss filled with unspoken emotion. She wanted to weep, knowing that when this was over, Iris would return to Secure Watch, and she'd have to go on with her life without the woman she loved. The idea of loving Iris after only a few days left her off-kilter, but that didn't change the truth. She had never felt this way about anyone in her life, and not just sexually. The emotions that filled her were startling, but every single one felt right. "Thank you for trusting me," she whispered, caressing her cheek before dropping her hand. Iris smiled with a nod. "Before starting on the computer, we need to eat something. I want to wash up, so let's go to my apartment."

"You go ahead," Iris said, trying to sit. "I should get started on this while Cal is at Walter's."

"No." Bec set the computer on the desk. "It will be there when we're fueled and rested. Besides, if Cal doesn't find a charger at Walter's, we may need to rethink how we do it so we don't waste too much battery power."

She could tell Iris didn't want to, but she finally agreed and followed her downstairs once she promised they wouldn't take too long to eat. After letting Declan know where they would be, Iris set her tablet on the table and turned to her.

"You clean up while I cook. We have a lot to do yet."

"Other than the computer, which may not tell us anything, we're waiting for everyone else to give us information. Let's use that time to shower and eat." Bec walked backward while holding Iris's hand, even as she tried to pull her to a stop.

"But what if Cal calls?"

"He'll call back," she answered, turning the shower on to warm once they were in the bathroom. Then she walked to Iris and kissed her, stopping the stream of excuses falling from her lips until the only thing she heard were moans of pleasure. In a flurry of arms, they stripped each other of their shirts and bras before Iris sat. Bec pulled her shoes, braces and pants off before she helped her into the shower.

Walking without the braces was dangerous as she noticed Iris often tripped on her toes, so Bec had her sit on the plastic chair she'd taken from the break room for Iris to use. Once settled under the warm spray, Bec stripped off the rest of her clothes, wrapped her arm in the plastic wrap and joined her, pulling the curtain before she leaned down to resume their teasing kisses. Water warmed them as they explored each other's bodies, almost allowing her to forget the reason why they were together to begin with. Almost.

Standing behind Iris, Bec massaged shampoo through her short blond hair until she tipped her head back and her mouth fell open from pleasure. Taking advantage, Bec walked back to the front of the chair and straddled her, kissing those open lips as the water rinsed their hair. Iris found the soap and lathered it, running her hands over Bec's body, teasing and taunting her until she came apart in her arms. Iris's lips absorbed her shuddering gasps as she floated back to earth.

"Anyone ever tell you that you have magic hands?" Bec asked, treating Iris to the same torture once she could move again.

"It's never been my hands that were the issue," Iris answered, moaning as Bec caressed her breasts, moving aside so the water could rinse them before she suckled a nipple.

All talking ceased as Bec showed Iris all the ways she cared about her without caring about any of her issues until the water cooled and she accepted that they had to rejoin reality. Once the water was off, she dried Iris head to toe before helping her out of the shower to sit on her bed. She wrapped her in a blanket and then carried her braces back to her.

"Could you please check the tablet and see if we missed any calls?" Iris asked, so she hurried to it and pressed the power button.

"Nothing yet," she answered.

They dressed in silence, and then she pulled a chair out from the table and motioned for Iris to sit before she pulled out cold cuts, cheese, bread and chips and set them all out on the table. She returned for water before sitting across from the woman she had just made love to in a way she'd never done with anyone else. There was something intoxicating yet soothing about their time together. Like the outside world, and all the fear that came with it, disappeared and they could find peace with each other.

"Thank you," she said, squeezing Iris's hand as she reached for a piece of bread. "For indulging me when your brain told you to do anything but."

"Before I met you, I doubt that would have been possible. It's not easy for me to stop in the middle of a task and not obsess over getting back to it. My neurologist says that's typical after my kind of brain injury. My therapist says it's typical of someone who's afraid or fears change."

"Who do you think is correct?" Bec asked, taking a bite of the ham sandwich she'd made while they talked.

"They both are, to a degree. My brain was injured, but I found comfort in the routine. Soon, I came to depend on it to feel safe."

"I'm glad you feel safe with me," Bec said with a smile, but Iris wasn't looking at her to see it.

"Never said I did," she answered instead, taking a bite of her sandwich.

"You didn't have to. The fact that you're sitting at my table talking to me about it shows me you do."

"Don't you want to know what happened to me?"

"Yes, but I promised Selina I wouldn't ask. That said, I don't need to know what happened to you to know that I like you for who you are now."

Iris kept her eyes pinned to the table as she chewed. Bec could tell she was uncomfortable, but she didn't say anything. It was okay to be uncomfortable in a safe environment. That was the only way to grow and find healthy ways to process trauma.

"It was my uncle. He kidnapped me when I was seven."

"Iris, you don't have to tell me," she said, reaching for her hand. "We're under enough stress as it is. Don't stress yourself out more."

"What if I want to?" She glanced up so quickly that Bec almost missed it, so she was glad she was smiling when she did. "There's no one alive but my therapist who knows the truth now. Sometimes, I think I could help people if I discussed it more."

"What does your therapist think about that?"

"She agrees but also knows how hard I've worked to be able to function at the level I do. She would never advise me to do something that could set me back."

"That's fair. As a clinician, she wants you to keep progressing in your recovery, not regress."

"The thing is," Iris said, catching her eye for longer before she stared at her sandwich. "I've been stuck in the same place of my recovery for years. Remember when I said my therapist says I'm afraid of being afraid? She's right. Whenever I think about telling someone the truth about what happened or try to think about what using my story to help others might look like, the fear gets too strong to overcome."

"Iris, look at me," Bec said firmly, waiting several minutes in silence until she lifted her head to look into her eyes for a quick moment. "You're stronger than your fear."

"No, you don't understand—"

Bec held up her finger. "Were you scared to come here?"

"Terrified, but I had to do it. You needed help, and so did Cal."

"Which is why I say you're stronger than your fear. The right motivation makes the fear worth it sometimes."

"Never thought of it that way. I've always thought that talking about it would hurt me again, and I feared that."

"How would it hurt you again? The emotions would cause too much anxiety?"

"You're going to laugh and think I'm dumb if I answer that."

Bec stood and knelt beside her chair. "I would never do either of those two things, Iris. You are the strongest and smartest woman I've ever met, and I've met a lot of strong, smart women. Whether you tell me anything more about your past or you never say another word, that won't change how I feel or think about you."

"I believe that," she agreed, staring at her hand on her thigh. "The truth is, for the longest time, I worried if I talked about what happened, he would come back and hurt me."

"Since you were seven when it happened, that's understandable, Iris."

She sat there, nodding and staring at her lap, until Bec stood, kissed the top of her head and sat back down at the table. "He's been dead since the second month of his prison sentence, though. The obvious answer is that I'm afraid of what happens after I tell someone the truth. Will you hate me? Will you think it was my fault? Will you not want to be friends with me anymore?"

"I wouldn't do any of those things, Iris, which I know is easy to say but hard for you to believe and trust. You were a child, so none of it was your fault."

"That's true. Everything I know about what happened before I was taken came from my mother. She had put me to bed and showered while waiting for my dad to come home. She worked the late shift at the hospital, and he was normally home for dinner but had to work late. She finished getting ready for work, and when he came home, he stopped to kiss me on the way to the shower, but I wasn't there. My window was open, and they found footprints below it."

"You don't remember that part?"

"Thankfully, I don't. The doctor said the damage to my brain was the cause and not repression. There isn't a single day that goes by where I'm not thankful for that after hearing the truth about what happened. See, my anxiety and OCD are because of the physical injury, not the memories of it since I don't have many."

"I understand," Bec assured her.

"They suspected my uncle was the one who took me. He was my uncle by marriage, and my aunt was divorcing him. He hated our family and knew how much my aunt doted on me, so he took me to make them suffer. For two days, he beat and molested me until he heard sirens one night. Thinking he'd been found, he slammed my head into the concrete floor and took off, leaving me for dead."

"But you didn't die," Bec said, taking her hands across the table and holding them tightly. "You're a survivor."

"I'm lucky to be this functional, according to the doctors. I spent over six months in the hospital learning how to do just the basic things like sit up, walk and eat. Once I was released, we tried to get back to the business of living, but it was hard on my parents, both emotionally and financially. My dad took a new job working on an oil rig where he made a lot of money but was gone more than he was home. He died in a work-related accident that set us up for life, but it broke my mother. She was never the same, and when she was diagnosed with cancer when I was fourteen, she refused treatment. Said there was no point in fighting it."

"Oh, Iris," Bec said with a sigh, but she just shrugged her shoulder.

"I didn't know how to convince her that I was worth fighting for when I was the reason her entire life had fallen apart."

"No," Bec said firmly. "Your uncle was the reason her life fell apart. You were an innocent victim, just the same as her and your father."

"That's what my aunt tried to help me understand, too, once I went to live with her at fifteen. Different aunt, not the one he was married to." Bec nodded her understanding. "Anyway, she took care of me and made sure I got through a technical program for coding, then set me up with my first apartment and job. It wasn't long after that when she passed away. That was when the struggles kicked in, and I learned just how much people judged those who were different. I was so lucky the day I met Mina."

"How did you meet her?" Bec asked, taking another bite of her sandwich. She was glad the heaviness of her childhood story was behind them. Iris had told someone she trusted about what happened, and now Bec had to ensure she understood that her opinion of her hadn't changed.

"Mina was at the doctor with Hannah Grace one day when I walked in looking for a job. I was desperate to find something. I got a small stipend from the money left from my dad's settlement, but it wasn't enough to live on, and I'd been evicted from my apartment. The brain injury made it difficult to work somewhere if there were too many people in the same room or where I had to face the public. It limited what I could do and made finding work that paid a living wage extremely difficult."

"That's understandable. You probably would have qualified for disability?"

"Maybe, but my skills were second to none in the right situation."

"I can't argue with you there," Bec agreed with a wink.

"Mina overheard me asking the receptionist about a job, and when she said they didn't have anything, I got sort of upset. Not like yelling or anything, but I started crying and tried to run out. And, well, we both know I shouldn't run."

Bec chuckled and nodded, her heart breaking for this woman who had overcome so much in life only to suffer even more injustices.

"Mina helped me up, sat me in a chair and then handed me her card. She asked me if I had any experience in cybersecurity work." She paused and looked around the room before she leaned in and whispered, "I lied to her."

Bec gasped in feigned horror. "Iris Knowles lied about something? That was teasing, by the way."

Iris smiled. "I figured that out because your voice has a different lilt when you tease."

"Really?" she asked, and Iris nodded. "I never knew that. I learned something new about myself today. Thank you."

She squeezed Iris's hands as she started speaking again. "It wasn't an outright lie. I knew how to do the job but had no experience besides my initial training."

"Ah, that's what we call inflating the résumé. Everyone does it," Bec said with a wink. "Go on."

"That's pretty much the whole story. Mina found out I'd been evicted and was living in a hotel with all my belongings in my car. She told me to follow her back to Secure Inc. and gave me a room for the night. The next day, she hired me as one of their digital private investigators. Once she learned my skillset, I transitioned into doing more and more coding and hacking as we set up websites for clients. I still do some digital PI work when the need arises."

"The first time I met you, I knew you were a spectacular woman, and everything you told me solidified that opinion. Thank you for sharing your story with me, Iris. It means everything to me that you trust me with it. I won't let you down."

She lifted her head to hold her gaze. "You're not like, I don't know, disappointed or put off by any of it?"

Bec shook her head immediately, standing and walking to her, straddling her legs as she lowered herself to her lap. "Why would I be disappointed or put off? What you went through was horrific and the result of the kidnapping has changed your life, but it also shaped you into the woman you are today."

"Not everyone thinks that's so great," she whispered, not making eye contact until Bec tipped her chin back to face her.

"Look around you, Iris. Everyone you work with thinks you're great. They love you. So much that when Selina was treating my arm, she gave me the third degree and then threatened bodily harm if I hurt you."

"Your voice didn't change there, which means you weren't teasing about her threatening you, right?"

Bec shook her head. "I wasn't. She was dead serious

when she said it. My point is that the only person who hasn't embraced your greatness is you. Do I understand why? Yes. Do I understand that accepting yourself will be difficult or even impossible? Yes. Do I hope you'll one day believe that you matter to so many people and deserve happiness? Also, yes. You deserve to be happy, Iris. When you can grab even a moment of it, do it. I promise it's worth the little bit of fear you'll feel in doing it."

"For the first time in my life, I want to try," she admitted, smiling as she stared at their joined hands. "You've shown me that happiness comes in places you least expect." Then Iris lifted her head and held her gaze long enough to tuck a piece of hair behind her ear that had fallen from her braid in the shower.

"I couldn't agree more," Bec whispered before kissing her sweet, plump lips. Hopefully, it told her how happy she was to hold her in her arms. They were just getting to the good part when the tablet started to ring.

Chapter Sixteen

Breaking the kiss, Iris grabbed the tablet and hit the red button. "Secure One, Charlie."

"Secure Watch, India," she responded, and Bec could tell her attention was now solely on the tablet. Cal's muffled voice probably startled Iris, as it did her.

When Cal appeared on the screen, he wore a hazmat suit and a respirator. "We found something in the basement. I'll turn the camera so Bec can tell us what it is."

Bec gasped when the camera revealed a lab space in Walter's basement. "That's a class three biological safety cabinet," she said without hesitation. "What is it doing in his basement?"

"I was hoping you could tell us," Cal said from behind the camera.

"Those are well over twenty grand, Cal. I don't know why he'd have one in his home. They're used when working with biohazards or dangerous pathogens that can't become airborne."

"Like viruses?" Cal asked.

"Yes. Usually, when working on gain-of-function research," Bec agreed.

"What's that?" Iris asked.

"Gain-of-function research helps us understand how

pathogens adapt to environmental pressures. That allows us to plan better disease control measures and explore vaccines and therapies."

"That sounds dangerous were it to fall into the wrong hands," Cal mused.

"It is," Bec couldn't help but admit. "If gain-of-function research fell into the wrong hands, it could be used for biological warfare without question. That's why this facility is secretive. Having security around us would make us an obvious target, but we also need to protect ourselves from bad players."

"Which is why Walter saying in the interview that you have the deadliest virus in your lab was risky," Iris deduced.

"It was, but now I wonder if he did it intentionally. Maybe he was looking for an investor or to set up a bidding war once he had a working vaccine for Ignis Cerebri. Cal, can you pan the camera around the room?" Cal did as she asked until she said, "Stop. That cabinet. Walk to it, but don't open it. Does it say ultra-low freezer?"

"Yes," Cal answered. "Should he not have that, either?"

"Since they start at ten grand, it's not there to hold his beer," she muttered, and Iris snorted.

"I see a lot of lab equipment, too," Cal said, pointing out a centrifuge and other pieces they use in the lab at the facility. "Does Walter work from home sometimes?"

"Yes, but not with viruses. That's taking your life into your own hands. Not to mention your neighbors. The biosafety hood helps, but it's seriously lacking when you don't have the benefit of the rest of the lab's safety features."

"You're saying it's like driving in NASCAR without a helmet? You can do it, but you shouldn't."

"Essentially," Bec agreed, still laser focused on the freezer. "The only reason he should have any of that equipment there is if he's working with live viruses, which doesn't make sense. That's what this facility is for, and in the length of time I've been here, he's never once entered a lab."

"What's in the freezer if it's not drinks?" Iris asked in confusion.

"Viruses." Saying it aloud sent a shiver down Bec's spine.

The camera flipped, and Cal filled the screen again. "Are we in danger by being down here?"

"Not from what I can see. The hood is clean, and there weren't any open vials inside it."

"There's a layer of dust on everything," Cal interjected. "It doesn't look like it's been touched in at least a year."

"Is the freezer plugged in?" she asked, and Cal nodded. "Is it running?"

"Let me check." Cal walked back to the freezer and knelt, leaning behind the small dorm-sized refrigerator for a moment. "I can hear it humming, and the side is cool."

"That would make sense. Those freezers go as low as minus 112 degrees Fahrenheit."

"Why does something need to be that cold?" Iris asked, and Bec couldn't stop the nervous laughter from bubbling up.

"To protect humankind from some very nasty pathogens. Cold storage allows labs to keep viruses and bacteria safe and alive until they need it for experimentation. Then they thaw whatever portion they need to conduct whatever test they're doing."

"That still doesn't explain what Walter is doing with it in his house," Cal said. "What if I open the freezer?"

"I want you to, but you must follow my directions closely, okay?" Bec asked, and Cal nodded. "Turn the camera around to face forward and have someone else open the door. Once the initial cold escapes, hold the camera down so I can see any printing on the vials. Do not get your hands anywhere near the inside of the freezer. When I say close it, whoever opened it should close it with their foot."

"Is it safe for Lucas to open it with an ungloved hand?"

"Yes, but once it's been opened, that plastic will get cold, so I don't want him to close it that way. With any luck, it's empty."

"And if we aren't lucky?" Cal asked. "Well, I guess I can puzzle that one out for myself. Ready when you are."

She said okay once the camera was forward facing, and Lucas, a Secure One operative, opened the door. Inside was one vial rack with four vials standing upright. "Can you get closer?" she asked, and Cal zoomed in on the vials. As soon as the recording stabilized, she gasped. "Close it."

Lucas's black-booted foot struck out to close the door as Cal flipped the camera around. Iris put her arm around her shoulders to help quell her shaking.

"What did you see?" Cal asked.

"Four vials and one said IC."

"Ignis Cerebri," Iris deduced, and she nodded.

"There's no reason for him to have a vial at his house.

His *house*," she said, emphasizing the word in a way that said it didn't belong there.

"Is it fair to say Walter's behind whatever is happening?" Lucas asked from where he stood next to Cal, both still wearing respirators.

"More than fair to say," she agreed. "Did you find anything else?"

"The place is wiped clean," Cal said. "When he left here last, he didn't plan to return. At least not for some time to come."

"But he left viruses there unsecured," she said, vibrating with anger.

"I'm hoping he returns for them," Lucas said. "Something tells me if he saved a vial of it, he plans to backstab whoever paid him to make the vaccine by turning around and selling more of the virus to someone else. Total warfare tactics."

"We've got the place covered in cameras. We installed a system that will lock him in if he shows up. I want to have a word with the good doctor."

"I want to do more than talk to him," Iris growled.

"Easy now," Lucas said with a wink. "You put all your anger into sorting out the computer. We did find a charging cord. Did you get past the password?"

Bec cut her gaze to Iris, who, thankfully, was nonreactive other than shaking her head. "Not yet. I was hungry, so we're grabbing a sandwich, and then I'll get back to it."

"You do that while we secure the house. We'll head back to the facility in under an hour," Cal said.

"I think you need to get out now." Bec took the tablet from Iris. "He may know you're inside or have left that vial there for someone else to pick up. Someone else, like a terrorist organization, and they won't care that you're the good guys. Unplug that freezer, get out and get back here, please."

Cal glanced at Lucas before answering. "Unplug the freezer? Won't that damage the samples inside?"

"Absolutely." Bec laughed, and even she thought her laughter sounded deranged. "It will kill the samples and render them useless to anyone. They're trapped in the vials and won't escape, and the viruses will be dead by the time anyone finds them. You can thaw viruses, but it must be done by slowly returning them to room temperature. Anything else means the pathogens will die a fast death. Unplug it." She paused and then tipped her head side to side. "Actually, don't unplug it. Just turn the dial on the freezer to off. If he does show up and notices it's unplugged, he might plug it back in. He'd have to check the dial to see that it isn't working, which he won't do. He'll just assume it is. Once you do that, get back here. I know you're security guys, but you're no match for terrorists."

"Fair point," Cal conceded. "It would be great if you have something for us to run down when we arrive."

"You got it," Iris said. "Come on up once you've sorted things there. I'll hopefully have the rest of the answers we need to find Zafar and Walter before this goes any further."

"Ten-four, Charlie, out."

The screen went black again, and Iris lowered it to the table. "You're a bad influence on me, Rebecca Roth. I just lied to my boss."

"Technically, you lied to Lucas, but I accept the title of bad influence if I get another shot at you in the shower."

"Now you're trying to get me fired!" Iris exclaimed.

Bec laughed loudly and hugged her, loving how her curves wrapped around her own. Everything that happened over the last few days had been unexpected, but Iris Knowles was the most unexpected. Her chest squeezed when she remembered they had so far to go yet, and when it was over, a life with Iris was not guaranteed.

She pulled back and traced Iris's lips. "What's the smile for?"

"I realized that since I got here, I've been able to let my guard down and make some jokes. That's never happened before," Iris admitted.

"Maybe you feel comfortable enough here to be yourself."

"Because of you, I'm sure," Iris agreed.

She didn't care that they were racing against time to find her boss when she leaned in and took her lips. The kiss turned heated the moment their lips collided. Bec took the lead, twining and cuddling their tongues until they were panting and had to break for air. Iris leaned her forehead against hers, something she noticed she did to maintain intimacy without forcing eye contact. Bec didn't care. It was a connection she craved, and she would take every last second of it until this was over and they could find a path to help them stay together.

"We should go upstairs and face Walter's computer," Iris whispered. "I don't want to drop the ball for Cal."

"I agree," she said, kissing her nose before unhappily extricating herself from the embrace to put the food away.

Bec desperately wanted the computer to be empty and just as desperately wanted it to answer all their questions.

One meant Walter was innocent and in danger, and the other meant he was guilty but safe. On second thought, neither was a great option. Oh, Walter. What did you get yourself into?

They'd made their way upstairs by the time she finished her internal debate. Iris turned the computer on, and the screen waited for a password. She tried 1234 and got nothing. Then she tried 0000. Still nothing. "Any idea what it might be? There are ways around it, but they suck a lot of power and time."

Bec pondered the question. "Try Ace." Iris typed it in, but again, it returned to the screen, this time also displaying a password reminder: *Sagacity.*

"Doesn't that mean understanding?" Iris asked, and Bec nodded.

"Yes, but it also means wisdom or knowledge."

"Could it be the college he attended or a professor's name?" Iris asked, but Bec stared at the screen with her head tipped to the side for a few more seconds before she pointed at it.

"Try cerebri."

Iris typed it in, and this time, the home screen loaded. "You're amazing!" she said, her fingers clicking on the trackpad as she opened the utilities.

"It made sense. Ignis Cerebri is a virus that burns the brain. What are you doing?"

"I'm turning on the battery saver. By doing that, our battery power will be extended. As long as we don't need the internet, we should have—" Iris glanced down at the corner of the computer "—about an hour before it goes dead. By then, Cal should be back."

"Okay, but where do we start? Files?"

"That would make the most sense, but see this?" She hovered the cursor over a cloud icon. "That's OneDrive." She clicked it, and when the app opened, she ran the cursor down to something called Personal Vault. "I'm betting the information we need is here, so let's begin. It requires a password. We only get ten tries before we're locked out. I would guess he doesn't know that the same password that opens his computer also opens this." She typed it in and sure enough, the vault opened.

"How did you know that?" Bec asked, pulling a chair next to Iris so they could see the screen.

Iris glanced at her for a second. "It's my job to know these things, but also, doesn't everyone know that?"

Bec held her hands by her chest as a silly grin lifted her lips. "I'll admit that I didn't know that either."

Iris shook her head in disappointment. "I'm going to let this one go because you'd be surprised how many people don't know how to utilize their OneDrive folders properly. Though, I'm sure you have programs you use for the lab with their own cloud."

"Yes, that," Bec agreed, feeling less out of touch now. "We only save to the cloud. I'm surprised Walter saves to his OneDrive. Maybe this is just for his home computing?"

"I would say it could be, but why did he have it in a secret compartment if it were? That doesn't make sense." She clicked open the files, but they all seemed innocuous to Bec.

"Those are all files for running the facility itself," Bec said, pointing at the spreadsheet Iris had just opened. "Maybe he kept the computer hidden so it didn't fall into the wrong hands should the facility be overrun. We don't want our operations information to be used against us."

Iris didn't answer as she continued to click files open and read them as though Bec didn't exist. Usually, she'd feel slighted by being ignored, but she knew Iris wasn't doing it to dismiss her purposefully. She was lost in her own world of computer language.

"You're concerned by what Cal found in Walter's house," Iris finally said, still searching the computer.

"There's no reason for him to have a biosafety hood and vials of the virus, Iris. That's how things go bad very quickly."

"I got that impression when you insisted Cal get out of the house."

"We don't know where Walter is, but if he was kidnapped by someone trying to get the virus, he could tell them he had a vial at his house. I don't want Secure One there if they show up. I can't believe how wrong I was about Walter. I've even had dinner at his house, and he was hiding that in the basement the entire time."

"Wait. When you started working here, where did Walter tell you he got the virus from?" Iris asked, taking her hands off the keyboard.

"He never actually said," Bec said, rubbing her temples. "I assumed this was one of the government projects we were working on. According to the literature I was sent, the lab has worked on government contracts in the past, and I didn't think it could be anyone else. Now, I'm not so sure, but it's not like I can call to ask."

"You're not sure because of the vial in the basement?" Iris asked to clarify.

"That, and looking back at all the times I asked him

who was backing the research so I could note it in my paperwork, he just kept saying use dot gov until the bureaucracy decides what they want."

"You're right. That is a strange answer. You weren't suspicious?"

"It felt weird, but I had bigger fish to fry with this vaccine. I told him we had to decide on it soon because I'd need to publish the first paper if we would continue to be funded. I thought the government was funding us at the time, so I followed their guidelines. Why didn't I ask more questions?" The sentence sounded more like an exclamation than a question, but Iris squeezed her hands until she felt calmer.

"You had no reason to believe you were being deceived," Iris pointed out. "We don't know that it's not the government fronting this research, so keep that in mind. We do know that Walter kept some of the virus for himself, so we need to find out why."

Shaking her head, Bec glanced up at the ceiling before she told the woman she'd come to care so much for what she knew for sure. "Baby, the only reason Walter would have a biosafety cabinet like that is if he worked with the viruses himself. Those other three vials in the freezer were the base mutation viruses for Ignis Cerebri."

Chapter Seventeen

Iris tipped her head in confusion for a moment. “Wait, you’re saying Walter created Ignis Cerebri?”

Bec nodded slowly, her lips drawing into a thin line. “I want to know why. Why was I deceived? Am I that gullible? What is wrong with me? I should have done more research, but my research and the people I talked to said this center was cutting-edge. It might look like a sleeper facility, but it was doing big things.”

“Were they wrong?” she asked as she returned to the computer to keep working. She didn’t have time to waste in case the battery died.

“Not about it being a sleeper facility and cutting-edge. I can’t say the part about doing big things. I’ve only worked on a project steeped in controversy and deceit. I should have seen this as a too-good-to-be-true situation,” Bec chastised herself. “Why would anyone hire me to create a vaccine for a yet unknown virus? Why wouldn’t they hire an entire team to do that?”

Iris turned to her again. “Did you know you’d work alone when you took the job?”

“No, not exactly. I knew I would be the head scientist in charge of gathering the data and directing workflow. I expected there to be others who would contribute, like medical, clinical and public health microbiologists, all working together to look at it from every angle. Once I arrived, Walter told me only one lab tech would be available to help me."

"And you believe you should have suspected that whatever was happening here was nefarious and walked away?"

"At the very least, I should have demanded more answers. Instead, I dove in headfirst, spurred by the very real threat of what another pandemic would do to the world."

"Fearmongering is real in any form, Bec. If you were led to believe that a vaccine was necessary sooner rather than later, it makes sense you would buckle down and get to work to solve the problem. Don't beat yourself up because you tried to do good and help millions of people from possible demise. Hindsight is always twenty-twenty, which is why it's called hindsight."

Bec's laughter was soft when she leaned in and rested her forehead against Iris's. "You're right. It's easy to see now that I was afraid of not being good enough or not measuring up because of what happened when I was a kid."

"Let me tell you what Mina told me when I started working for Secure Watch and felt the same way. She said they tell us as kids we can be whoever we want to be but show us the exact opposite is true by dictating what we can be and when. We can't change our past, but we can shape our future by being who we wanted to be as kids. Who did you want to be then, Bec?"

"Myself," she whispered. "I just wanted to be myself.

Someone who helped others, was kind, made a difference and was happy in my skin."

"You help others, are kind and make a difference. The question is, are you happy in your skin?"

"Yes. Since I met you, I've never been happier, Iris."

"Me, too," she whispered, leaning in to kiss Bec's lips. "So let's work the problem together. No more blame game, okay? Cold, hard facts, just like if this was a science problem you had to solve."

Bec sat up with a smile. "You're good at tough love, Iris. I'll give you that. Okay, no more pity party. Let's solve this problem so we can get on with our lives."

Iris turned to the computer, but the screen before her swam as she blinked back the tears that filled her eyes. She couldn't let them fall and risk Bec noticing that she was upset. It wasn't as though she didn't know they'd go their separate ways when this was over, but having her confirm it broke her heart. She tried to tell herself how important it was that she learned she could love someone, but her heart didn't want to hear it.

Clearing her throat, she focused on the files, running her finger down the screen without looking at the wonderful, intelligent, gorgeous woman beside her who could never be hers. "Do any of these names sound familiar?"

"No," Bec answered immediately, as though she'd already been reading through them.

"They aren't abbreviations for diseases or anything?"

"I guess they could be, but I wouldn't know what without opening them all. If I saw H1N1 or HEV, I would know they were viruses, but that's not what these are."

"Then we open them," she said, clicking the first one. However, the file was empty, as were the next six.

"How can they all be empty?" Bec asked, leaning in close enough that her floral scent tickled Iris's senses, adding to the sadness already engulfing her.

"Red herrings?" Iris asked, clicking out of the file and hitting the start button before clicking all apps.

"What are you looking for?"

"An app that fronts as something else but is a vault for files and photos. Something tells me Walter wasn't as bad at technology as he led you all to believe."

"That's becoming apparent," she agreed while shaking her head. "He had me fooled, though."

"No, he kept you busy. There's a difference. He could say whatever he wanted, but you were too busy to see what he was doing." She paused for a moment and then grinned. "There you are."

"What?"

Iris clicked on an app, which brought up a password box. "Folder Hider. A classic app for hiding and encrypting files."

"Do you think the password is the same?"

"The hint for this one is Ignis plus Cerebri," Iris said, pointing at the words under the empty password box. "I doubt he'd make it the same."

"Brain burning," Bec said instantly.

With a tip of her head, Iris typed in the two words but was told it was the wrong password.

"Add a hyphen. He always added a hyphen to the two words when he wrote it out."

Iris added the hyphen. This time, the box opened, revealing files and pictures that weren't encrypted. She opened the first file and clicked through pictures taken of Walter and his setup in the basement.

"It looks new in these pictures," Iris pointed out, and Bec nodded.

"Maybe he took them to prove he had a system set up?" Bec asked as Iris kept scanning through them. At the end, there was a video, and Iris clicked Play.

"As you can see, I'm more than prepared to meet your organization's needs. The lab is complete, and I'll await your specifications and go ahead." Walter spoke to the camera as though he was addressing a specific person or place.

"It's dated one year ago," Iris said, pointing to the date of the video.

"This explains why the other scientist didn't know what Mina was talking about when she mentioned Ignis. He hadn't made it yet. I was the sucker he brought in to make the vaccine for it."

"Why would they need a vaccine for it if they're terrorists?" Iris asked. "That part confuses me."

"Simple. They don't want to die. They'll take the vaccine and protect themselves and those they love while sentencing everyone else to death."

A shudder racked Iris at the thought. "We know that Walter set the lab up at someone else's request, so now we need to find out who that was. If I were Walter, I'd want a contract, right? Let's see if we can find one."

She clicked open several more files, but Bec shook her head each time, telling her they were information about the base viruses she had seen in the freezer at Walter's house. None of it told them why he was mutating a new virus or for whom. After ten minutes of searching, Bec blew out a frustrated breath.

"Maybe he didn't have a contract or never uploaded it."

"There had to be a contract, but maybe it's smarter to follow the money trail. Mina said he went from being deeply in debt to being debt-free almost overnight. Unless she discovers a rich dead relative, it's a bit suspicious."

Bec snorted, but it wasn't out of amusement. "Walter doesn't have a rich relative."

"My gut says the same unless his rich relative is very much alive and very much a bad player. So far, we have proof that he set the lab up at someone's request. There has to be another file here to tell us who—"

A loud bang made them both jump. "What was that?" Bec asked.

Iris grabbed the walkie-talkie. "Secure Watch, India." She released the button and waited but got no response. "Secure Watch, India!" She waited but still didn't get a response. "Something's wrong, Bec."

"Let's give them a minute in case they can't stop doing what they're doing to respond."

Her heart pounding, she closed the laptop and set it aside, grabbing the tablet to call Cal when the stairwell door slammed open.

"Thank God," Iris said, but the rest of the thought died on her lips.

Four men, dressed head to toe in black with only their eyes showing, marched into the lab, assault rifles aimed at them as they approached.

"Who are you?" Bec asked, putting herself between the men and Iris. "You have no right to be here."

"Walter sent us," one of the men sneered. "We're here for Ignis."

"You can't take a dangerous pathogen out of the lab. That's suicide."

"He said you completed the vaccine," another one said from the left.

"Completed, yes—proved its effectiveness, no. That will take years."

"We'll take our chances," the first guy said. "Open the door to the lab."

Iris shook with fear as the men aimed their rifles at them, making it almost impossible to think about what to do next. Were Declan and Zac alive? Had they been hurt? Had Cal arrived yet? Cal! The thought penetrated her terror, and she leaned over to cough, hoping it didn't sound fake. While bent over, she hit the panic button under her shirt, alerting everyone at Secure Watch that she was in trouble. If Cal was still at Walter's or headed back, he'd know they needed help.

"Where's Walter?" Bec asked. "I won't do anything until I talk to him."

"We'd like to know the same thing," the ringleader said. "We've been trying to reach him since he missed our scheduled call. We're not waiting any longer."

Was Walter planning to double-cross them by taking off and leaving Bec holding the bag? It was starting to look that way to her.

Slowly, Iris stood up, enraged at the thought that her friends could be hurt or worse. "What did you do to my friends?"

"Relax. They're fine. Or they will be once they wake up from their little nap and find a way to untie themselves. We aren't here to hurt anyone. That includes you. As long as you do what we say."

Iris could hear the hint of an accent but couldn't pinpoint where it was from. Bec reached behind her and took her hand, squeezing it.

"What do you want us to do?" Bec asked, and the guy motioned to the lab with his gun.

"Open the lab door, but don't make any sudden moves."

Bec nodded. "I'm going to turn around and explain to my friend what she needs to do on the computer so I can use my metrics to open the door. I'm not trying anything. We've had some computer difficulties. Not everything is working properly."

"Hands where we can see them," he responded, and Bec raised her hands before she turned to face Iris.

"You're okay?" she asked, and Iris nodded, her eyes wide. She wasn't okay, but she didn't want to freak Bec out and make her worry when she had four guns aimed at her back. "I'm going to need you to go through the sequence just like last time so I can enter my biometrics at the door."

"But Bec, that's dangerous."

Trust me, she mouthed, and Iris snapped her lips shut, even if they continued to tremble as she faced off with the woman who had taught her so much about herself in such a short time.

"Just sit down slowly and wait for me to get to the lab door, then type everything in exactly as you did last time."

Bec turned around, and the guys walked her to the door, where she waited. Iris was confused because she didn't need her to open the door. Since she didn't know what she had planned, she sat down and typed away on the laptop as though she was doing something important. She occasionally glanced at Bec, who had moved to the side while the guys lined up in front of the lab door. She kept typing, hoping to buy time in case Cal got her SOS alert and was on his way.

"Come on already, we don't have all day," the ringleader growled.

Bec gave her a nod, so with shaking hands, she hit the enter key dramatically. The woman Iris realized she had big feelings for entered her biometrics and waited for the door to slide open. From there, everything happened at once. The door opened, and Bec pushed the men into the room, sidestepping the ringleader as he yelled, but she didn't get him into the room before he looped an arm around her neck and dragged her backward, training his gun on Iris.

Chapter Eighteen

"Don't hurt her!" Bec yelled, but her words were strangled from the chokehold she was in.

"You should have thought about that before you decided to play games!" The ringleader yelled, red-hot anger tightening his arm around her neck.

She put her arms up in the "don't shoot" position. "I'm sorry," she croaked. "I'm scared."

Iris sat in the computer chair, her arms up in the air, but they trembled so much they fell limply to her lap. She shook violently, and tears fell down her cheeks as she locked eyes with Bec for a brief moment. Bec could read the terror in them. She had to defuse the situation, but she had no idea how.

"Boss," another guy said as he walked out of the lab. "There's nothing in there."

"Where's the virus?" he asked, tightening his hold on Bec's neck.

She couldn't answer because black dots filled her vision and she struggled to breathe. She clawed at his arm until he finally released her enough for her to suck in air. "I destroyed it!"

Iris gasped from across the room and brought her

trembling fingers to her lips, the fear in her eyes telling Bec she understood the pickle they were in.

"You did what?" he growled, dragging her backward toward the lab. "What about the vaccine?"

"I told you the vaccine isn't finished! It's in pieces and parts that need to be tested." That wasn't true, but he didn't appear to be the kind of guy to understand how vaccine research worked. She had a vaccine, but it wasn't proven yet. The dose she had wasn't enough to use, even if it was safe to use.

"Then you'll get the pieces and parts," he grunted. "You're coming with us."

"No!" Iris said, jumping to her feet.

A shot rang out, and Bec screamed as Iris went stock-still for a moment before dropping to the floor.

"You shot her!" Bec screamed, trying to run to Iris, the fear in her gut telling her in that moment that she was in love with her, but the animal kept hold of her.

"The shot went wide," he said, laughter filling the room. "She's being dramatic."

"She has anxiety and PTSD from a kidnapping when she was a child," Bec spat. "I need to check on her."

"You'll do no such thing," he said, walking her toward the lab. "You'll tell my men where to find the vaccine, and then you'll come with us."

Bec's entire body froze at his words. "What do you want me for?" she asked with fake bravado. "I don't know anything about what's going on here. The government hired me to work on a vaccine and nothing else."

"You were hired to work on a vaccine, but no one said anything about the government. My employer bought and paid for that virus and sent us to collect it."

"It's not here!" she exclaimed again as he tightened his arm around her neck.

"That's okay. We have the next best thing—someone who can recreate it. If we can't find Walter, at least we have you."

A glance at Iris, still unmoving on the floor, told Bec what she had to do. "The vaccine is in the small freezer on the left of the hood. They're marked V1 and V2. Put them in the small red cooler next to the freezer."

It was a lie. There was no vaccine since she had turned off the freezer and let it thaw after she destroyed the viruses kept in a separate part of the lab. Thankfully, she had left the vials in the freezer until they had thawed. It would have been hard to keep this ruse up if she hadn't done that.

The ringleader motioned for one of the men to do as she said, and once he returned with the cooler, they pulled her down the long hallway.

"Iris!" she screamed, clawing at the guy's arm as she tried to free herself to run to her. "Iris! You have to wake up! Iris!"

As the door to the stairwell closed, the beautiful, vibrant woman remained crumbled in a ball, and Bec was afraid it was the last memory she'd ever have of her.

Iris blinked several times as she awoke, a fuzzy snout licking her cheek. Lucas's PTSD dog, Haven, was nuzzling her with his nose when her eyes came open.

"Iris," Cal said softly from where he knelt beside her. "We got your SOS."

SOS? Had she activated her panic button? Why did she feel wrung out as though she'd run a marathon? That only happened after an intense panic attack. She sat up and glanced around, the lab coming into focus until the memory of Bec in that guy's arms and the gun going off ran through her mind.

"No, no," she cried, frantically searching the room as her heart rate went from normal to off the charts, and her limbs once again felt like lead.

Someone lifted her arms and wrapped them around Haven's neck. "Haven is safe," Lucas said in a calm, even voice. "No one can hurt you now. Take some deep breaths so you don't pass out again," he coached, and she tried to do what he said, but her chest was paralyzed by the thought that those men had taken Bec.

"Be-be," she stuttered, trying to form the words and tell them what happened, but her panic made that impossible. She couldn't speak. Her heart felt like it was going to explode, and the dots in her vision were getting worse by the second. Burying her face in Haven's fur, she tried to breathe with him, but nothing was helping. All she could hear was the gun going off and then the way Bec's face filled with terror.

"I need to get to her." Iris heard Selina's voice, and she lifted her head to see Haven posturing to keep her safe.

"Haven, friend," Lucas said, and the dog lowered himself back to the floor and looked up at her under his bushy eyebrows.

"Iris, open your mouth. I'm going to put this under your tongue. It's an extra dose of anxiety medication." Selina held a tablet, so Iris opened her mouth without thinking or questioning. The tab went under her tongue, and she prayed it worked quickly. She had to help Bec.

"Are you hurt?" Selina asked, but Iris just shook her head. "Let's get her into a chair."

Cal and Lucas helped her into the desk chair, where Selina checked her blood pressure and pulse before handing her an ice pack to hold to the goose egg on her head. She must have hit it on the floor when she fainted.

"Did B-Bec activate her panic button?" Iris finally managed to ask.

"Not yet," Cal said, squeezing her knee.

"Zac and Declan!" she exclaimed, trying to fight her way up, but Selina and Cal held her in the chair. "They're tied up downstairs!"

"They're fine," Lucas said, moving Haven next to her and resting his head on her lap. Then he put her hand on his head and encouraged her to pet him. She did because his head was soft and warm, soothing her jangled nerves. "They're both nursing headaches from being knocked out but are otherwise okay. They said they were jumped and never saw the guys coming."

"We didn't, either," Iris admitted. "We heard a loud bang, and those guys were here before I could get anyone to answer on the walkie-talkie."

"Who are they?" Cal asked. She could tell he was trying to be patient with her, but it was hard for him.

She inhaled a deep breath as the antianxiety med started to lessen the adrenaline in her system and allowed her to think. "We don't know who they were. There were four of them, and they wore all black and had assault rifles. They wanted us to let them into the lab to get the virus because they couldn't reach Walter, and he missed their phone call or something like that."

She waved her hand in the air in confusion before blowing out another breath.

"They were looking for Walter but couldn't reach him, so they came here?" Cal asked, and she nodded.

"Yes. I think Bec was going to try and trap them in the lab, but the one guy who was mean grabbed her around the neck and wouldn't let her go. He got meaner when the other guys couldn't find the virus."

"Where did it go?" Lucas asked in total confusion.

"Bec said she destroyed all the viruses. She must have done it while I searched Walter's office for the computer."

"What happened to make you pass out?" Selina asked, squeezing her shoulder.

"He shot her!" Iris exclaimed, tears running down her face as Haven whined and put his paw on her lap. "He shot her."

Selina grasped her chin in her hand and shook it gently. "Iris. There's no blood anywhere in the lab. Are you sure you saw him shoot her?"

With great difficulty, she met Selina's gaze. Her eyes said she wasn't lying. She paused, trying to sift through the fear to find the truth.

"The gun went off," she insisted. "But I'm not sure where the bullet went, truthfully. I thought he shot her, and I passed out from a panic attack."

Lucas stood and walked around the work area while they continued to talk to her.

"Without blood, it's safe to say Bec wasn't shot," Cal said. "The question is, where is she?"

"They took her!" Iris moaned the words more than she said them. "Right before I passed out, they told her to get the parts of the vaccine that she had left because she was going with them."

"Did they say why they wanted her to go with them?" Cal asked.

She shook her head. "No, but I can only assume it's because they think she can either recreate the virus or get Walter to cooperate with them."

"Boss," Lucas called from behind her. "Found the bullet, but I don't think this printer will print another day."

"Oh, thank God," Iris said, her shoulders slumping in relief. "We have to find her!"

"We will," Cal assured her. "I'm holding out hope that she activates that panic button sooner rather than later. If only we knew how long she's been gone."

"Does it tell you what time I activated the panic button? I was probably conscious another five minutes before he fired off the shot."

"Great thinking!" Cal said, grabbing his tablet and calling it up. "She's probably been gone thirty minutes, which seems like a lot of time, but in this part of the country, you can't get far in thirty minutes. That said, we don't know what they're driving, so until she hits that panic button, we have no choice but to wait."

"What? No!" Iris exclaimed, trying to stand but being forced back into her seat. "We can't wait! We have to call the police. They can find her!"

"And what am I supposed to tell them?" Cal asked gently. "That a woman has been kidnapped, but we don't know by who, what they look like, or what they're driving? I'm confident that Bec will activate that SOS button as soon as possible. Do you know where she kept it?"

Iris's cheeks heated before she answered. "I showed her how to hide it in her bra."

"Good," Selina said, patting her shoulder. "Less chance of anyone taking that when doing a body search."

"I tried to remember what Cal taught us," Iris agreed.

"If they tied her hands behind her back, then she might need to wait until she can convince them she needs the bathroom before she can activate it. Let's be patient. If they took her and the vaccine, they want something from her, so they're not going to hurt her."

"I hope you're righ—"

Cal's tablet rang, and he glanced up at them. "Mina," he said before he answered with their traditional greeting.

"I've got a bead on Walter," she said without preamble. "His phone pinged at a cabin about thirty minutes from your location yesterday."

"Yesterday? Had it been off before then?" Cal asked, and Mina nodded. "I wonder why he turned it back on."

"For the call," Iris said without hesitation. "Maybe the coverage isn't good, and the call didn't go through, but he had to know those guys were going to call."

"I was thinking he was checking to see if the ransom had been paid early," Mina said. "What call by what guys?"

Cal filled Mina in on what had happened and that Bec was taken. "Send me the coordinates for the cabin. They're likely gone, but on the off chance they're still there, I need to check it out. Keep an eye on Bec's SOS button. If it goes off, notify me immediately, and I'll change course. Did you find a deed for the cabin? Do you know who owns it?"

"Walter," Mina answered without hesitating. "It appears he bought it last year around the same time he paid off all his other debts."

"That's not a coincidence," Lucas said, to which Cal agreed. "What direction is the cabin? His house is only about thirty minutes from here, too."

"It's south of you instead of north like his house."

"I predict we find Walter's belongings there, but he'll be long gone. Regardless, we're on our way."

"Ten-four," Mina said. "But wait, Iris, do you know if Bec has her phone on her?"

"I don't know," Iris said, leaning forward. "Let me call it."

"No!" Mina exclaimed, holding out her hand for calm. "If she has it and you call, that could alert them." She held up her finger and typed on her computer before she spoke. "I'm running a check on it. It last pinged off a tower about ten miles from your facility. Hasn't pinged since."

"Coverage out here is extremely hit and miss," Cal said.

"Or they took it from her and tossed it," Iris said, her lips in a thin line. "Come on, baby, you gotta activate that panic button."

"She will," Selina promised, squeezing her shoulder while Cal and Mina finished their conversation.

"Selina, would you stay with Iris? I'll let Zac and Declan know we're heading to the cabin. Efren and Mack are doing patrol, so I'll leave them here. Lucas will come with us."

"I'm going, too," Iris said, standing from the chair.

"That's unnecessary," Cal said, holding his hand out to her. "This is just a quick check to see if Walter is there. It's probably a waste of time, but we can't assume they're already gone."

"If he is there, I have a few words for him," Iris said between gritted teeth. "He's put Bec in danger and needs to answer for that!"

Cal held his hands out to her as though that would calm her.

Think again!

"Iris, it's better for your health if you stay here with Selina."

"I can't sit here and do nothing!" she exclaimed. "I'll stay in the car, but I want to go."

Cal's gaze darted to Selina, who shrugged her shoulder. "There's little she can do here, and it might help her anxiety if she has something else to focus on."

Cal sighed and put his hand on his hip. "Fine, but you stay in the SUV and do whatever I say without questioning me."

Iris saluted him, which lifted his lips in a half smile before he turned on his heel and headed to the stairs. She offered Selina a grateful smile before she followed, praying that they would find Walter at that cabin and the woman she couldn't wait to hold in her arms again.

Chapter Nineteen

The engine roared as the driver gunned it across the highway onto a dirt road. Bec wasn't sure how long they'd been in the car, but she was disoriented from the blindfold they'd strapped over her eyes as soon as they were out of the facility. The only part about the blindfold she liked was that it meant they didn't want her to see where they were going. That meant they didn't plan to kill her immediately. She took some comfort in that while she tried to figure out her next move.

When they pulled her out of the center, she hoped they wouldn't check her for a phone, but she should have known that was too good to be true. They chucked it out the window onto the side of the road, never to be seen again. Unfortunately, all she could think about was Iris crumpled on the ground. She hadn't seen any blood, so she didn't think she'd been shot. Sure, the megalomaniac who took her said he shot wide, but she couldn't be sure of that. Her heart had stopped beating for that moment when Iris gazed at her with so much fear and then collapsed. Was it likely she'd had a panic-induced fainting spell? Yes, but there would be that little niggle of doubt in her mind until she saw her again. If she saw her again.

No. When *I see her again.*

It wasn't easy to stay positive, but she had to for Iris's sake. There was no way she'd put her through the trauma of losing someone else in her life, not after she had been so open and honest with her. What Iris went through since she was seven was cruel and brutal. All she wanted to do was be her resting place and carry some of the burdens for her. Without a doubt, her employment at the research facility was over, so whatever she did after this, she would make sure it worked for both her and Iris. She didn't intend to give her up if they ever got a chance to be together again.

First, she had to get out of this alive. The only way to do that was to give these guys what they wanted—a deadly virus and a working vaccine. She wasn't doing the first, and there was no way she had time to do the second, which meant she had to convince them she could do both without doing either. She bit back the anxious laughter bubbling up from within as the car slowed to a stop. One of them opened the hatch of the SUV where she'd sat for the entire ride. With her hands and feet tied, it made staying upright difficult, but she'd managed by leaning against the back seat after she wedged herself into the corner. The blindfold was ripped from her eyes, which shocked her until she realized they were still wearing their masks, so she couldn't identify them. Now that they'd reached their destination, it didn't matter if she saw where they were. A quick glance out the window told her it was a small cabin in the woods.

Dragged from the vehicle, she immediately fell to the gravel driveway. "My legs are asleep," she muttered when they ordered her to get up. "I can't feel my arms or my legs. You need to untie me."

"So you can run? Not a chance in hell." The guy she had started to call RL, short for Ringleader, was the one who spoke.

"Then someone better carry me inside." Her bluster got her fireman carried into the cabin before they tossed her onto a couch, where she landed with an *oof*, shooting pains filling her body as her arms twisted painfully behind her. "Hey!" she yelled, nearly falling onto the floor. "If you want me to be able to use my arms to help you with your little problem, they're going to need to work. Can't you at least untie my wrists? If my feet are still tied, I can't go anywhere. If I don't get blood flowing in them soon, there will be permanent damage."

RL cut his gaze to her. "Fine, but don't try anything."

"Again, where am I going to go?" she asked as one of the guys closest to her snapped the flex-cuffs apart. Her shoulders screamed in pain as her arms fell to her sides, but she didn't let them see it. She just rubbed at her wrists as she leaned back against the couch to rest her tired back.

"What now, boss?" one of the guys asked.

"We bring a virus and working vaccine back to the client. I don't care how long it takes."

"How? We're missing the scientist who can make the virus." One of the guys hooked a thumb at her. "She can make the vaccine, but that's useless if we don't have the bug."

Bec cleared her throat and followed it up with an eye roll. "You realize I can create an even deadlier virus than Ignis Cerebri, right? All Walter did to get it was basic gain-of-function research. He mutated other viruses and changed their DNA profile to create something deadlier than any could be alone." She was throwing out every term and idea she could think of to confuse them in hopes they'd decide she knew what she was talking about. In truth, she did know what she was talking about and could recreate Ignis Cerebri, but they didn't know that. To them, she was a vaccine creator only.

"Wait," the ringleader said, turning to face her. "You can create the viruses, too?"

"I hold a PhD in cell, molecular, health and disease biology. Of course, I can create a virus."

"My boss wants Ignis Cerebri yesterday and is running out of patience."

She remained quiet, wondering how she would pull this off. Only Walter had the information for making the virus, and she had no idea how he did it or how long it took.

Walter!

"What if I told you I knew where to find another sample of Ignis Cerebri?"

"I'd say I'm listening," RL said, walking over to her.

Internally, she smiled. She had him right where she wanted him.

Iris was more than pleased when she realized that Cal had an SUV rather than a UTV to ride in. She had climbed in the back and prayed that Bec would be at the cabin when they arrived. Logically, she knew that wasn't likely, but a little piece of her heart wanted to hold on to it, so she allowed it. Maybe Walter had turned his phone back on to call the guys who took Bec and they were having a rendezvous. She didn't want anyone to get hurt, but she desperately wanted to find Bec.

Cal slowed as his navigation system told him they were approaching the road where the cabin was located. He'd pushed the speedometer over eighty miles per hour to cut their trip time, but now it was time to proceed with caution and not show their hand to anyone who had Bec. Iris was hanging on to the idea that they'd taken Bec because she had the knowledge and experience to recreate Ignis Cerebri and give them the weapon of mass destruction that they'd paid for. She would never do it, but they didn't know that. Iris suspected Bec would let them think she would for as long as she had to so they could find her. Why hadn't she activated that SOS button yet?

Iris's phone started to ring, which surprised her, considering how spotty the coverage was. She saw Mina's number and answered immediately. "Secure Watch, India."

"Secure Watch, Whiskey," Mina said. "Bec hasn't activated the panic button yet, and her phone hasn't pinged again. Where are you?"

"Nearing the turnoff to the cabin," she answered, her heart sinking to know Bec was still off the grid. But then she reminded herself that those guys needed her alive if they wanted a working virus. "Would you do me a favor while we're checking out the cabin?" she asked, and Mina agreed. "See if there's a lab facility within a reasonable driving distance of where we are. Maybe a private lab or hospital?"

"To what end?"

Iris hesitated momentarily until she remembered the fear in Bec's eyes when the gun went off. "The guys said their employer had paid for Ignis Cerebri, and they'd come to collect it. We know they took her to recreate the virus, so to do that, she'd need a place to work. It would have to be somewhere with access to virus samples because she would need that to make the new one."

"I'm not sure it's possible to waltz into a lab and demand access to deadly viruses, Iris," Mina gently said. "That's not legal."

"That didn't seem to bother these guys when they broke into Bec's lab and kidnapped her at gunpoint!" Haven nudged her with his nose, reminding her that he was there and she was safe. Lucas sat beside her and squeezed her shoulder as Cal glanced in the rearview mirror. "Sorry, Mina," Iris said. "Please don't fire me."

"I'm not going to fire you," Mina assured her. "You do make an excellent point. If they want her to recreate that virus, and that's the only reason to take her, they're going to need a lab and samples to do it. Assuming they don't have their own set up somewhere."

"I hadn't thought of that," she agreed, chewing on her lower lip. "Why hasn't she activated the panic button?"

"Could be a lot of reasons," Mina said to calm her. "Give her time. Maybe she forgot about it or hasn't been able to do it discreetly yet. It can't hurt to look for labs within driving distance of the research center. I'll do that while I await your assessment of the cabin."

"Thanks, Mina," she whispered before she hung up. When she glanced up, she noticed the car was silent. "I'm sorry for yelling. I'm so worried about Bec."

"Completely understandable," Selina promised from the front seat. "It's not easy when someone you care about is in danger."

"I know it feels like we won't find her, but we will. I believe she will activate that button as soon as she can.

Once that happens, we'll call the police and get her rescued," Cal assured her.

"But you said the police will just muck everything up and put people's lives in danger. We can't risk that," Iris said, grabbing the front seat.

"I did say that," Cal agreed calmly. "But when I said it, we were in a different situation. When you're talking about a hostage situation, we'll have to involve the police. There aren't enough of us here to get her out safely. We'll need SWAT, at the very least, depending on where they take her. One thing at a time," he said, turning left onto a dirt road. "Let's see if Walter is at the cabin."

"What's the plan, boss?" Mack asked from the back seat. He'd insisted on coming along for extra backup. Iris appreciated that.

It was beyond pitch-black now that they were off the highway. With clouds obscuring the moon, even the headlights barely made a dent in the darkness that surrounded them. All too soon, Cal switched those off, too. They would have to approach on foot on the off chance Walter and Zafar were at the cabin.

"From what I can see, we're about as far as we dare go with the car," he answered, pulling to the side of the road. "We all go in on foot, but Selina and Iris hang back with Haven once the cabin is in view."

"We could wait in the car," Selina suggested, but Iris objected.

"No. I want to be there if Bec is inside."

Cal shook his head. "Selina, I know your shooting skills are superior, but I don't think it's a good idea to leave you here with Iris unprotected. If it was just you, I'd say you can hold your own, but not if you're worried about her. We all go. I expect this to be a wild-goose chase, but regardless, I want you to cover the road approach while we check the cabin. If something moves, shoot it. Clear?"

"Ten-four," Selina said, opening her door.

They left the SUV, and Haven jumped down to follow Lucas out before she and Mack followed. She took deep breaths, concentrating on the image of Bec's face in her mind after she'd made love to her. Happy. Sated. Maybe there was a touch of disbelief that they could feel that way about each other when they had just met. The truth was that Iris knew everything she needed to know. Bec was her due north, and if—no, when—they found her, she vowed to find a way to be with her. She didn't know if she could leave Secure Inc. and follow Bec somewhere else, but for the first time, she wanted to try. The thought of being without her was harder than risking everything to be with her. There was nothing she wouldn't do to hold her again. Kiss her. Touch her. Spend her life with her. Her anxiety felt manageable when she was in Bec's arms. It would never be gone, but it was as though Bec agreed to carry a little bit of it for her so she could rest for the first time in twenty-six years.

As she picked her way down the road behind Mack, with Lucas and Selina bringing up the rear, she realized the changes she'd seen in herself in the last few days were astounding. She would always be neurodivergent and have multiple disabilities because of her brain injury—love couldn't cure that, but honestly, she didn't want it to. Those disabilities made her who she was and taking them away would have put her on a different path where she may not have met Bec. Would her life have been easier?

The short answer was yes, but she couldn't say that definitively. There are no guarantees in life, and anything could have happened at any time to make her life just as difficult. She thought about Bec, and the strength and fortitude required to leave her home at such a young age and trust people she had never met to keep her safe. The idea slowed her heart rate, and she inhaled deeply for the first time since leaving the car. Bec was going to be okay. She was smart and savvy, and she could think on her feet. All Iris had to do was trust her, just like she'd asked her to do before she opened that lab door.

Cal held up a closed fist when the cabin came into view, and they all stopped. Cal, Lucas and Selina dropped into a crouch, but she and Mack both had foot drop and couldn't do that. He lowered himself to the ground and sat, so she followed his lead. One light was burning from within the structure, which was clearly someone's old hunting cabin. She doubted there were more than two rooms inside, but that didn't matter if it was just a place to hide out until their gigantic payday sent them off to the tropics, never to be seen again. A car was parked to her right, and Cal motioned for Lucas to check it out.

He approached it silently, popping his head up to peer into the windows several times before he ran his hand across his neck as though to say, *no go*. It was empty.

Cal whispered. "Let's approach as though whoever is behind those doors is alive and well."

The three men walked toward the structure while Selina pulled her and Haven behind the car, her gun aimed at the dirt road they'd crept up. She planned to take Cal literally when he said to shoot anything that moves.

She heard the squeak of a doorknob and then silence.

The longer there were no voices, the more her heart sank. If Bec was in there, she would have said something by now, right? But then it hit her that there were no voices, not even those of the Secure One guys.

"Secure One, Charlie," Cal said as he came around the car and picked Iris up by her waist. He ran up the road, everyone falling into place behind them.

"Put me down, I can walk," she said, confused about what was happening.

"We have four minutes to get the hell out of here before that cabin blows," he said tightly. "This is a run, not walk, kind of situation."

Before she could reply, she was shoved in the back of the SUV as everyone piled in behind her. She tried to right herself as Cal whipped the SUV and slammed the accelerator. She had no sooner buckled her seat belt than a loud blast blew her back in her seat.

Chapter Twenty

"What the hell happened back there?" Selina asked, turning to take Iris's hand. "How are you doing?"

"I'm worried about Bec," she admitted. "I have to assume she wasn't in the cabin."

"She wasn't," Cal said tightly.

Selina dug into the bag at her feet and sat up with a bottle of water and a pill.

"What's that?" Iris asked, her head cocked in confusion.

"Another dose of your anti-anxiety medication."

"I don't need it but thank you." She did take the bottle and cracked the lid, gulping some of the water. "Thanks. I haven't had anything since lunch."

"You're handling this very well. I'm proud of you."

She held her head high and made eye contact with her friend. "Thank you," she said.

"Was anyone in the cabin?" Selina asked, turning back in her seat.

"Walter," Cal said with a nod. "Another person I can only assume was Zafar. Both died relatively recently, but there were no guns, so they weren't self-inflicted or murder-suicide. It looked like they'd been surprised and dropped where they were standing. The door was still unlocked, which was how we got in."

"Anything else of interest?" Selina asked.

"You mean other than enough C-4 to blow three cabins that size?" Mack asked, to which she snorted.

"Yeah, other than that."

"There was a computer on the desk," Cal said. "It had the message up that Ace sent to the computers at the research facility. That confused me because how was there internet way out there?"

"There was coverage, though," Iris said. "Mina called me as we turned down the road."

"Maybe that's why Walter bought that cabin," Selina mused. "He knew they'd need to use a hotspot to send the message through."

"The bomb is confusing," Lucas said. "It was attached to the door, so if it was opened again, it would blow, but five minutes on a timer gives someone plenty of time to leave. Case in point, us."

"It does," Cal agreed, "but if the cabin and the bodies get blown sky-high, there's no evidence to collect even if someone does report it."

"But wait," Iris said, her mind trying to link together everything she knew so far. "The guys who took Bec said that Walter missed their call. If he's been dead this whole time, that means they didn't kill him."

"Nope," Cal agreed.

"That means there's a third player in the game, right?"

"Most likely," Lucas said. "Our guess is Walter decided to double-dip."

"Like he took the money from the employer of the

guys who took Bec and then set up the ransom? But why?"

"It's possible the employer of the guys who broke into the facility figured out he planned to double-cross him and had him killed, then sent the guys to get what he was owed," Cal explained. "We need to get back to the research facility and secure it. With Walter dead and Bec missing, it's time to call someone in to take control of it."

"Not until we find Bec!" Iris exclaimed. Haven raised his head, and she took a deep breath before speaking again. "We need to find her, and we need to find the evidence on Walter's computer that says she's not behind this. We need proof of her innocence once we find her."

Cal nodded as they neared the research center. "I've had Delilah tearing apart the computer while we were here. I'm hoping she has a report when we get back. If she doesn't, it will be your job to help her while we wait to get a bead on Bec."

Cal's phone rang, and he hit the phone button to answer it. "Secure One, Charlie."

"Secure Watch, Whiskey," Mina said. "Did you find Walter?"

"We sure did," Cal said, filling her in on their discovery. "I didn't want to call you until we were clear of there."

"I guess you can let the board president know the money won't be needed when he arrives later tonight."

"Wait, the president of the board is arriving tonight?" Iris asked from the back seat.

"Considering they currently have no one in charge of the facility under their employment, they thought it prudent to secure the viruses safely."

"There aren't any viruses," Iris said. "Bec destroyed them all once she could get back into the lab."

"Well, that's something," Mina said with a sigh. "All the same, it's their right to take control of their business."

"Did they give you an ETA?" Cal asked, checking his watch.

"His flight lands in Grand Forks at 2100 hours. It's another hour and change to the research center."

"That doesn't give us much time to find Bec, but if they kick us off the property, we'll set up a base at the motel in Sinlis Park."

"He's coming alone, so I doubt he'll kick you out unless he picks up an entire security team along the way. That said, I wouldn't talk about anything around him that you don't want him to know. I sent Delilah his name and information. It will be waiting for you to read through when you arrive. I'm also keeping an eye on Bec's panic button. So far, it's still quiet."

"Ten-four. Charlie, out."

He hung up the phone and sighed. "Just what we need. More people to muddle the mess we already have."

Lucas was on his phone and finally hung up as the lights of the research center came into view. "That was Zac. It's been quiet since we left. They're expecting us."

Iris let out a breath to hear that news. She didn't want her friends to get hurt again, and the last thing they needed was another round of unnamed goons to surprise them. Once the car was in Park, they all climbed out to stretch. Lucas and Mack stayed to fill Zac, Declan and Efren in on what happened at the cabin while Cal and Selina ushered her into the facility and up to the lab. With any luck, Delilah had found something on

Walter's computer that would help them sort out who might have Bec.

That low buzzing of anxiety sat in Iris's belly as they stood in the elevator. She didn't know if it was because she was afraid Delilah hadn't found anything or that she had. Maybe her worry for Bec was catching up to her. Once the doors opened and everyone stepped out, she held Selina back while Cal went ahead.

"I was maybe wrong to turn down that extra dose of meds."

Selina dug in her pocket and pulled out the tablet, popping it out of the packaging into her hand. "Right under your tongue. It's not a big dose. Just enough to take the edge off." She rubbed her back several times while she waited for it to dissolve. "It's only been three days since you left Secure Inc., but I can see a fundamental shift within you."

"Bec has taught me a lot about myself in a short time," Iris agreed. "Like the fact that my therapist was right all these years."

"About what?"

"That a lot of my anxiety is based on the fear of talking about what happened to me and being judged for it. When I told Bec, and she didn't judge me, it hit home that I'd had control all along."

"Wait. Bec promised me she wouldn't ask you about it."

"She didn't. It was my choice to tell her. She told me I didn't have to, but I wanted to help her understand what happened to me."

"That's impressive, considering you've never told any of us," Selina said with a head tilt.

"Let's be honest, Selina. Mina knew what happened to me thirty seconds after running a background check. You all know."

"Fair, but you've worked for Secure Watch for years and have never uttered a word to any of us about it. You've known Bec for three days. That's my point."

"When Bec trusted me with her story about leaving the Amish community so young and how difficult that was for her, it made me want to be equally honest with her about my past. My therapist told me years ago that not talking about it allowed me to stay caught up in the fear where it felt safe."

"The fear felt safe?"

"To me, yes," Iris admitted. "At least everything I kept around me because of the fear. Some of my compulsions and intrusive thoughts were tied to keeping everything a secret."

"Do you know why?" she asked, and Iris nodded immediately.

"Fear of being judged. I think you can probably understand that, right?"

Selina's chuckle filled the hallway as she nodded. "I spent years being someone else to avoid being who I was. Granted, there was a mobster who wanted me dead, but even if that hadn't been the case, like you, I found safety in keeping my secret safe inside. Being honest meant running the risk of losing someone else in life when they learned the truth."

"Until you meet the one person who doesn't make you feel like that would happen."

Selina flashed her ring finger. "I married that one person."

"If I can find her, I just might do the same," Iris said with a grin. "I don't know how it will work, but if I ever get to hold her in my arms again, for the first time, I want to try."

"That's so wonderful to hear, Iris," Selina said. "We all deserve someone in our life who makes us feel like we can slay dragons, and if we can't, they'll do it for us."

"There's that," Iris admitted. "Since love doesn't cure my disabilities."

"No, but when it's real and true love, it doesn't care about your disabilities."

"And that's what Bec has taught me," Iris agreed. "We both know I'll always have anxiety and OCD. That's part of my brain's pathology now, amongst other things, but what she's shown me over the last few days is that my therapist was right. If I work hard, I can find a way to live my life without being on edge every second of the day. Once I put the effort in of confronting what happened to me and how it shaped me, a lot of the anxiety I carry about that event will fall away, and what I'm left with is easier to treat since my fight-or-flight response is not constantly assailing it."

"That's incredibly self-aware, Iris. Everyone at Secure Inc. will be proud of you. Bec will be, too. For putting yourself in the back of an SUV just in case you'd find her in a cabin where the risk to yourself was great. She'll be proud that you didn't give up on her."

"Never," Iris said. "But I should have realized it would get the better of me eventually. It always does."

"No," Selina said, holding her out by her shoulders. "The fact that you get up and fight every day to work and be part of our family says something else entirely.

Baby steps, Iris. You're stressed in a new environment and worried about someone you care about. You're upright and fighting through it, which is impressive. I'm here for you, and I'll be here for Bec when we bring her home. We will bring her home."

Iris nodded once, the tension in her belly releasing from Selina's encouragement. She didn't have to be afraid of being afraid. That was compounding the problem. Don't try to block the fear. Feel it and then put it to use. She remembered the hundreds of times her therapist told her that and suddenly understood what she meant. Blocking out half of the fear let her focus on the part she could do something about.

"Now, lift that chin, and let's go find your girl," Selina said with a wink as they walked into the workspace.

Chapter Twenty-One

When Iris and Selina entered the workspace, Delilah had Walter's computer open on one of the high tables with a writing pad next to it. She and Cal were conferring but turned to them when they walked in.

"Hi, Delilah. Thanks for helping with this," Iris said, hugging her friend.

"Not a problem, sweetie," Delilah promised, patting her back. "I've found some interesting tidbits I was just telling Cal about, and we both think Walter had some big plans."

"What did you find?" she asked, walking behind the table to look at the computer.

"From what I can tell, Walter had no intention of giving the virus to only the group who commissioned it."

"Do you know who that is?" she asked, and Delilah held up her finger.

"We'll get to that. I want you to read this and tell me if I understand it correctly."

"Delilah, you worked for the US Government as a cybersecurity expert. You have far more experience than I do."

"All the same," she said, motioning for her to read through a document on the screen.

"It looks like a standard contract of goods to me, with Mr. A as the buyer and Mr. W as the seller."

"Okay, that was my thought, too. Now—" she held up a finger and brought up another document "—read this one."

Iris read it several times before she flipped back to the other contract. "It's the same contract, but it just says Mr. X as the buyer."

Delilah held up her finger and pulled up yet another one on the screen. This one had Mr. L as the buyer.

"Are you telling me that Walter planned to sell Ignis Cerebri to three different people?"

"Or countries," Cal said.

"It could even be different viruses," Delilah said. "According to Cal, he had four samples in his basement freezer, correct?"

"Yes, but according to Bec, some of them were the base for Ignis."

Selina shrugged. "All that means is he had one massive bioweapon and three smaller ones."

A word fell from Cal's lips that described exactly how she felt. "That means we have three potential bad guys all looking for a virus promised to them by someone driven by greed."

"And one of them has the woman I love, so we need to tear this place apart until we find their names and where they call home," Iris said, her hands in fists at her side.

"I'd argue, but she's not wrong," Cal said. "Are there dollar values on these contracts?"

"No," Delilah said with a frown. "They read that the agreed upon fee will be paid at delivery."

"Shouldn't that be on a contract?" Selina asked as

she leaned on the desk. Iris could tell the long days were catching up to them, but they couldn't stop until they found Bec.

"Oh, I'm sure it's on the final contract. This is probably an early one before all the specifics were worked out. As you see, they aren't signed."

Iris turned to Cal. "You guys went through his house, and there was nothing there?"

"Nothing," Cal said. "The place had been wiped clean other than the vials in that freezer. According to Bec, they had to remain in a deep freeze, which meant he couldn't take them with him. He probably planned to get the ransom and then return to his house long enough to get the viruses to fulfill the contracts. Chances are, the final contracts are in a safety deposit box somewhere."

"How much money did this guy need?" Selina muttered.

"But wait," Iris said, waving her hand. "There's something here that doesn't make sense, or should I say someone."

"Someone?" Cal asked, and Iris nodded.

"Bec. Why bring her in to make a vaccine when Walter knew the virus would have to go to the buyer long before she could make a working one?"

The room fell silent other than Cal tapping his fingers on the table. "Hadn't thought of that, but you're right. It doesn't make much sense to promise a virus and working vaccine to someone and then not give the scientist time to make said vaccine."

"Unless there's another player," Selina said. "A legitimate one."

"You mean one who wanted Ignis Cerebri for evil and one who wanted it for research like Bec thought?"

Selina pointed at her with a nod. "Bec doesn't know what happened before she arrived, only after. So if the original requestor of the research was dealing with Walter, it would be easy for him to see an opportunity to capitalize multiple different ways on it."

Iris considered that until she remembered something. "But Walter had that video on this computer." She held up her finger and then found it again, pressing Play for them to watch.

"Okay, but he just says to fulfill their needs," Cal said. "That doesn't mean he was referring to Ignis Cerebri. For all we know, he could have made other viruses. The video was uploaded a year ago, but we don't have the actual date it was recorded. It could have been long before he uploaded it."

"True, and if that's the case, it's safe to say they aren't the ones who stormed in here and took—" Her tablet started ringing, and she jogged to her desk to grab it.

"Secure Watch, India," she said when she saw Mina's name on the screen.

"Secure Watch, Whiskey," Mina answered. "Bec just activated her panic button. She's headed toward Sinlis Park!"

BEC LEANED AGAINST the back of the couch while she waited out her captors. They were hard at work looking for a lab to overtake so she could "do her work" with the virus. Maybe she didn't know who their boss was, but she knew they were afraid of him. They'd been clear that they'd better return with the virus and vaccine, or they would be pushing up daisies.

She couldn't figure out why Walter would promise them a virus *and* a vaccine when he knew that vaccine research takes years, not months. Sure, she'd developed one over the last five months, but it was an early attempt, and the final version wouldn't even resemble the current one by the time it was finished because that's how it worked. Trial and error. Tweaks and changes. Not that it mattered now. Ignis Cerebri was dead, and it would stay six feet under if she had anything to say about it. Thankfully, these boneheads didn't know that, so she had the element of surprise on her side. Maybe it was the element of deceit on her side, but either way, she would use it to get out of this jam. First, she had to let them get good and frustrated with finding a place for her to work.

No matter how she looked at it, she couldn't make any of it make sense. Walter was a scientist and knew how virology worked. Since none of the other scientists Mina spoke to knew about Ignis Cerebri, she could say with certainty that he didn't roll it out until she took the position five months ago. Was that on purpose? Did he want as few people as possible to know about it? Then why mention it in that interview? She thought about the date of the interview, and it hit her. That interview was long before Ignis existed. Why would he say that if he hadn't even created Ignis yet?

Her breath caught in her chest. This wasn't the first time he'd made and sold deadly weapons to people! That would explain why he went from deep debt to debt-free almost overnight. He hadn't used a prepayment—he'd used payment from selling a different virus to a different organization. Most likely, one who planned to use it for warfare. Fury rose in her chest at the man who had duped her, and at herself for being so gullible. Iris had said Bec couldn't look at it that way because she acted in good faith. That was true. She had interviewed with Walter, and the board had accepted her application and credentials, though she had never met anyone on the board. She didn't think that was unusual since they were spread around the country on each coast. That was why they had Walter in charge of the facility.

Bec realized it didn't take him long to figure out how that benefited him. He could do just about anything he wanted as long as he made it look to the board like everything was on the up and up. When no one was checking on the facility regularly, it was easy to alter paperwork and make it say one thing while you did something else entirely. That was how he had pulled all of this off. She had to give him credit if that was true. It wasn't easy to fool people in their community, but he'd done it many times over to multiple scientists. That also made her feel slightly less bad about her part in it.

What buoyed her spirit was knowing that she could do something about it now to end his reign of terror and prevent deadly viruses from falling into the hands of the wrong people. It was frightening that she even had to think that, but in the day and age of cyberwarfare and bioweapons, it was a realized fear. She shuddered to think what would have happened if she hadn't called in Secure Watch.

The thought gave her pause. Why had he let her call in Secure Watch if he was behind what was happening? Why would he demand ransom from the board when he was making millions or even billions selling viruses to terrorists? She replayed the scene that morning where Walter was "kidnapped," and it hit her. The bullet that had broken the glass in Walter's office wasn't meant to scare her off. It was meant to kill her. Calling Secure Watch didn't matter because he planned for her to be dead by the time they arrived. Secure Watch would walk in and find her on the ground, dead from a bullet, while Walter escaped scot-free. Red-hot fury filled her, and she leaned forward, ready to make her move.

"I know of a lab where I can do this work," she said, breaking into the conversation the guys were having.

RL turned to her. "Why didn't you say something before?" His tone was accusatory, but she simply smiled and shrugged.

"You'll have to forgive me, but being forcibly kidnapped and held hostage has slowed my thought processes. Listening to you just now, I remembered that the place where the viruses are also has a functional lab. It's rudimentary but more than suitable for my purposes." She leaned back smugly, though she kept her expression neutral for their benefit.

"You're bluffing," RL said. "How could you possibly know that?"

"I worked with the guy who owns the lab, that's how. I've been there. Call your boss. He knows."

All four guys glanced at each other until RL shook his head slightly. "We can't call our boss. If he finds out we don't have the virus, we'll be dead by morning, and so will you."

"Well, I, for one, want to get out of this situation alive, so I guess you're going to have to trust me with yours."

Another round of stares happened before the ringleader responded. "How far away is this lab?"

"Since I have no idea where we are, all I can say is in relation to the research center, it's about ten miles. It's in Sinlis Park."

"There ain't nothing in Sinlis Park, boss, much less another lab," one of the other guys said.

"Sometimes, sleepy little towns hide bigger secrets than you know, gentleman," she said.

"Will it hurt anything to check it out?" one of the black-clad ninja wannabes asked his leader.

"Only if it's a trap," RL answered.

"It's not," she answered immediately. "Only one other guy knows about it, and he's been kidnapped, so I assure you he's not there."

The guy turned to her slowly. "Walter Hoerman?"

"You guessed it. He has a full lab in the basement of his house. If you can get me in there, I can have your virus in a matter of hours." Man, she was rolling out the lies left and right. "I can have a tentative vaccine in twenty-four hours." Bec struggled to keep a straight face saying that bald-faced lie, but she did it. In her opinion, she deserved an Oscar.

"I know you're lying," RL said as he stalked toward her, striking fear through her. Was this it? Had she gone too far? "We searched Dr. Hoerman's house days ago."

"There was that one room we couldn't get into, boss." The goon's words made RL turn back to him. "Remember, no matter what we tried, we couldn't open that door?"

"A lead-lined door," she explained. "They're used to protect other areas of the lab, or in this case, the home, from radiation and viral escape. Very common." If she didn't stop all this lying, she would surely go to hell. It did make her wonder how Cal got into the room, but knowing Secure One, they had their ways.

"How are you going to get in, then?" he asked as if it was a "gotcha" question she wouldn't have an answer for.

"I know where the key is." At least, she suspected she did. "Listen, we can sit here all night and debate this, but the clock is ticking, according to you, and your boss wants his virus. So, what's it going to be?"

The ringleader turned back to the other three, who were all nodding, shaking their heads and shrugging as though they didn't know the correct answer, but doing nothing meant certain death. When he turned back to her, he smiled, the whites of his teeth jarring against the blackness of his mask.

"We'll do it your way, but one trick, and you're dead. Understood?"

"Completely," she agreed, saving her smile until he turned away.

She had them right where she wanted them. She patted her chest to check on her panic button. It was ready and waiting. She'd click it as soon as they were ready to leave, leading Secure Inc. right to Walter's door. Of the five in the room, only she knew that once inside, they weren't getting back out.

Chapter Twenty-Two

Her heart pounding, Iris gripped the tablet tightly. "Where is she? Can we intercept them?"

Mina shook her head. "Not unless you know what they're driving, which we don't."

"How far out are they from Sinlis Park?" Cal asked, grabbing his phone and texting someone while he waited for her answer.

"Twenty minutes, give or take," she answered. "I don't know that they're going to Sinlis Park, but that's the direction they're heading in. Intercepting them there is easier since they have to drive through the city to continue on the highway. It's almost 11:00 p.m., so it shouldn't be hard to pinpoint them once they're going slow enough that I can give you landmarks their vehicle is passing."

"That's assuming they aren't coming here," Cal said, and Mina tipped her head in agreement.

"That seems less likely as they have to know that by now, the research center has been locked down and the cops have been called."

"Walter's," Iris said, slowly turning to address Cal. "She's taking them to Walter's."

"Why would she do that?" Mina asked as Cal pointed at the tablet in agreement.

"Think about it, Cal. You found a lab in Walter's basement. They took her so she could create a virus, but the samples here at the lab were already dead. Now she needs more samples."

"But the ones at Walter's are dead, too," he pointed out. "She had me turn off the freezer."

"But they don't know that," Iris said with a grin. "Bec knows if anyone walks into Walter's, they're not getting back out until Secure One arrives."

"You could be right," he said, grabbing the tablet from her. "Mina, don't lock that house down once they're inside."

"I thought that was the point," she said in confusion.

"It was the point when the plan was to trap terrorists, not scientists. If they think for any reason that she set them up, they could kill her. I won't risk that."

"You'd better leave now then if you're going to beat them there. I'll patch you into her GPS so you can monitor their progress or in case they're just passing through."

Cal checked his watch. "We have a few hours until the board member arrives?"

Mina nodded. "I just checked, and his flight was delayed. Why?"

"I don't have enough people here to save Bec and keep the research center covered. I'll have to pull everyone over to Sinlis Park and hope it's not a trick."

"A trick?" Iris asked, more confused than ever. "What's a trick?"

"You mean that they aren't planning to return to the research center?" Mina asked, and he nodded.

"No," Iris said adamantly. "She's taking them to Walter's."

"You can't know that for certain, Iris," Mina gently said.

"I do know that because I know her!" she exclaimed, tears pricking the back of her lids. "Bec knows I'm here, and she would never endanger me by bringing those guys back here."

Selina grasped her shoulders in comfort. "We believe you, Iris. Just take a deep breath."

"Honestly, I'm with Iris on this one," Delilah said. "She was in the room when Cal told them anyone going in wouldn't get back out. She's counting on it."

Cal nodded once. "It's decided. We're headed to Walter's," he said, pointing at the camera. "Get that GPS patched in and shut down that security system. Call the cops and fill them in, then link them to my phone.

"On it. Whiskey, out," she said, and the screen went blank.

Everyone started talking at once until Cal whistled, and the room went silent.

"I'm coming with you," Iris said.

"Yes, you are, but only because we're abandoning the center. However, you'll be waiting at the motel with Delilah while the rest of the team heads to Walter's."

"Cal, no," she started to say, but he slashed his hand through the air.

"Listen to me, Iris. You are not qualified in any way to be part of this operation, and I can't be worried about keeping you safe while trying to save the woman you so obviously care about."

"You can say it. I love her, and that's okay."

Cal held up his hand. "It's wonderful, but that doesn't change the fact that your only experience with criminals is from behind a keyboard. When I have Bec safely in hand, Delilah will bring you over. Okay?"

She could see no point in arguing, so she nodded once. After grabbing her tablet, she followed the rest of the team to the elevator, which they rode in silence other than Cal barking orders into his phone as they descended. There was no doubt in her mind that Bec was leading those guys back to Walter's. She had every intention of being there to take her in her arms when she was freed and then never let her go.

BEC WATCHED AS the lights of Sinlis Park came into view. She was one step closer to making her way back to Iris. She just had to hold on a little bit longer. The car slowed as they pulled into town, and she took slow, deep breaths so she wouldn't overplay her hand. She had to get them into that house and get downstairs to the lab before they realized they couldn't get back out.

"You better not even think about double-crossing me," RL said from the driver's seat as he turned right and drove down the block where Walter's house sat. He drove around the block several times as all four craned their necks, looking for anything unusual.

"I have no reason to," she promised. "The sooner I make the virus, the sooner we can part ways. No one wants that more than I do." Bec said it like she believed they were going to let her go once she finished the virus. She wasn't naive. She knew they wouldn't, so she needed to lead these guys to Secure One's doorstep. She could have hit the panic button much sooner, but she had no idea how long the battery lasted on them. She needed to wait until Secure One had the best chance of finding her.

It still surprised her how well Secure One and Secure Watch worked together to protect their clients. Whether you needed cybersecurity, personal security or both, they were up for the job. Thank God for that, or this whole thing could have ended differently.

Still could, Bec. Don't get ahead of yourself.

With the reminder fresh in her mind, she took a deep breath. *Play it cool, Bec.* "If you drive around this block one more time, it's going to be you who looks suspicious," she said, hoping not to rile him up but to make him stop and think.

"She's right," the guy in the passenger seat said. "We either commit or get out of here. I haven't seen anything out of place."

The ringleader slowed the car and parked at the end of the block with Walter's house in the middle. He turned to the back seat and pointed at one of the guys. "You stay with her." Then he looked at the other two guys. "We do a sweep on foot. There's too much light here for the night vision goggles, so stay alert."

They exited the vehicle quietly with the dome light disabled so no one could see inside. When they disappeared, Bec worried her lip between her teeth as she waited. What made her the most nervous were the deadly assault weapons they still carried. If Secure One was waiting for them, someone could get hurt, and it would be on her conscience since she had led them here. At least they were familiar with Walter's house. There was less chance of an ambush when you knew the property than when you didn't, right?

"Bring her in," the radio on her guard's shirt squawked,

making her jump. "Remind her if she tries anything, we know where her friend lives."

Iris.

Bec swallowed around the lump in her throat. "I'm not going to try anything. I'm not in the mood to die tonight. I just want to make your virus and get out. I didn't sign up for this when I took the job."

The guard climbed out, making a show of slinging his rifle around as he walked to the back of the SUV and opened the hatch, motioning her out. He kept his gun pointed at her as she climbed out, and then he prodded her along with it. They stayed in the shadows, but she still couldn't help but think they better hope no one was looking out a window.

Once they were around the back of the house, the ringleader let them in the back door while everyone filed in, guns pointed as they cleared the house. It was empty, which relieved and distressed her at the same time. Then again, maybe Secure One wouldn't move in until they were locked inside the house, assuring them no one could get the jump on them.

"You," RL said, pointing at her guard. "Outside on patrol. If you see any cars, report back immediately." He reached for the door, and Bec held her breath. What happened next? Did an alarm go off when they tried to leave but couldn't? Did the door refuse to unlock?

It took her more than a second to register that he'd not only opened the door and let the guy out, but no alarm had sounded when he opened or closed it. What the hell? Something wasn't right, so she had to hope and pray that her panic button had transmitted her location.

"You. Downstairs," RL said, motioning her down

the stairs as soon as he flicked on his flashlight. It was treacherous, but she managed to get down the stairs.

"I'll need light if you want me to create a virus."

"Then you better hope that room doesn't have windows, or it's going to be by candlelight," he growled.

Bec grabbed the lab coat next to the door and slipped it on. It was miles too long for her, but she had to play the part. She stuck her hand in the pocket and pulled out a key.

"You mean the key was in the coat the whole time?"

"I assume so," she said, walking to the closed door at the end of the room.

He blocked her way with his gun, holding her back from the door as she put her hands up. "How did you know it was there?"

"I didn't," she said, her words wobbling slightly. "But it made sense. The first thing a scientist does is put on his lab coat, so I knew he'd have one here. Logic told me putting the key in the pocket meant he'd never lose it."

Still somewhat skeptical, he motioned at the door with his gun, so she stuck the key in and turned it, pushing the heavy door open to reveal the lab Cal had shown them. She was relieved when there were no windows in the lab. Instead, the vent of the biosafety cabinet went out the side of the house in what used to be the window. Walter really had her snowed. He cared so little about people that he endangered his neighbors with this setup. Sure, the cabinet had a filter, but filters fail, and then what? Obviously, Walter didn't care.

A small desk lamp sat on a table, and she snapped it on, taking in the room. She didn't need PPE since the viruses she'd be working with were already dead, but the meathead behind her didn't know that, so she had to make an effort.

There was a loud crash above their heads, and he turned to the door. Bec saw her chance.

"What was that?" she asked, feigning fear as she came up behind him.

"I don't know, but don't move," he said.

Too bad he didn't know she already had. There was one shot at this and one shot only, so she sent up a prayer and then grabbed the door and threw her body weight behind it, shoving him out of the room and locking herself in. She stumbled backward with a sigh and awaited rescue.

Chapter Twenty-Three

"Bec!" Iris screamed as Cal brought her out of the house. She was wearing a lab coat that made her look like she was wearing her daddy's clothes, but she'd never been more beautiful.

"Iris!" she cried, grabbing her in a hug the moment she was within reach. "Thank God you're okay. They wouldn't let me check on you after you fell. I wasn't sure if you were hit by the bullet or had just passed out from fear."

"Definitely the latter," Iris promised without releasing her. "I've been so worried but knew you could handle yourself. I'm so proud of you for playing these guys!"

Bec's laughter filtered into the ragged edges of Iris's heart and smoothed them out. They were both okay, and once they got this sorted out, they could be together. "Who are these guys? Did you find anything on Walter's computer?"

"You won't believe this," Iris said, leaning back to peck her lips with a kiss. She had to keep it short as there were too many cops around for PDA. "According to what we found on Walter's computer, there are at least three different—"

"Rebecca Roth?" someone behind her asked. Iris turned and came face-to-face with another cop.

"I'm Rebecca Roth," Bec said, stepping forward. "I suppose you have questions for me."

"You could say that," the cop said. "Turn around and put your hands behind your back." He took out handcuffs and opened them. "You're under arrest."

"For what?" Bec asked, following orders as she put her hands behind her back.

"Suspicion of murder and being an accomplice to a terrorist."

"What?" Iris asked, her voice an octave higher than normal. "You can't arrest her! She didn't do anything! This is all Walter's fault!" Strong arms grabbed hers as she was about to wade in and grab Bec away from the cop. "Let me go!" She tried to free her arms, but Cal's grip was too strong.

"Relax, Iris," he whispered in her ear. "You can't stop this from happening by assaulting a cop. That's going to land you in the cell next to Bec."

"But we can't let them arrest her! She didn't do anything, Cal!"

"We know that, but the cops know nothing right now. We need to get back to the research center and find all the information we can to prove Walter's guilt and her innocence. Without proof, they can hold her for as long as they want."

"No!" Her cry was plaintive as the cop led Bec away, sticking her into the back of a cop car. Bec pressed her forehead to the window and met Iris's gaze, fear filling her eyes. "You can't let them take her."

Cal flipped her around to face him. "Iris, listen to me.

I have no control over what the police do. I'm lucky we aren't the ones in the back of the cop car. Until we have evidence to show the police that Bec had nothing to do with this, she's at their mercy. That said, if she's in a jail cell, she's safer than at the center. We still don't know who all the players are in this game, and until we do, it's better if she's tucked away under the watchful eye of an entire police precinct. Let's stop wasting time here and return to the center. We have less than an hour before the board president shows up. That's not much time to find something to prove her innocence."

"If anyone can do it, you can, Iris," Delilah said, approaching them. "But is it safe to go back there, Cal?"

"I can't answer that," he admitted. "We still don't know who their employer is, nor do we know if there's anyone else out there looking for a virus they were promised. I want you to get that laptop and our equipment out of there before Mr. McCarthy shows up. I'm sending Lucas, Selina, Zac and Declan with you two. I have to stay here until this mess is cleaned up. Mack and Efren will stay with me. The guys who took Bec are long gone, but thankfully, we have them on our surveillance to prove to the cops Bec wasn't here willingly."

"Meeting up at the motel?" Delilah asked, and Cal nodded.

"The moment you have everything cleared out, get out of there. I don't want to be there when Mr. McCarthy shows up. He's worried because no one under his employ is in charge of the center, but I'm worried he will accuse us of something far worse. Mina will keep you posted on when he's expected to arrive. You should be long gone before that time."

"Ten-four. It won't take us long to pack up the computers and get out. She didn't bring much in," Delilah said.

Cal turned to Iris. "While she's packing the equipment, I want you to grab everything from Bec's apartment. Once we get her released, there's no telling when she'll be able to return to the center for her things. I'd prefer it if she didn't have to at all. Can you do that for her?"

Iris nodded quickly, her gaze darting to the street again, where Bec was still in the car. She'd turned away and stared out the windshield, tears on her cheeks. "She doesn't have much there other than her clothes. She told me most of her personal belongings were in storage. I won't let you down, Cal."

"More importantly, you won't let her down. Now go. Time isn't on our side."

Iris darted after Delilah, her drop foot braces barely allowing her to walk fast, but thankfully, Delilah was used to it and didn't push her to move faster than she could. Zac pulled up in Cal's SUV, and they piled in before he did a U-turn and headed back toward the highway. Iris couldn't get past the tears on Bec's cheeks, and one fell down her own, which she quickly swiped away. Now was not the time to fall apart. She had to keep it together for Bec. Cal was right. She was safe, and at least in jail, no one who had a grudge against Walter could get to her.

"There has to be another vault app," she muttered, staring out the window.

"What now?" Delilah asked, waiting for her to respond. "Another vault app?"

Iris turned to her. "Walter had to have used a cloud vault. One that he could access from any of his devices. A hidden computer isn't always convenient."

"That's true," Delilah agreed. "I didn't look for cloud-based vault apps on the laptop because I was so busy with the one already on the computer."

"A red herring?" Declan asked from the front seat.

"Could be," Iris said. "Either way, that's the first thing we look for once we have the computer again."

"I have the computer," Delilah said, a cheeky grin on her face. "I stuck it in my bag when we headed to Walter's. I didn't want to risk someone else coming in and taking it when the place wasn't under our protection."

"I should have thought of that." Iris grimaced. "Thank God you did."

Delilah patted her back. "Don't beat yourself up about it. You had other things on your mind. As soon as the guys clear the space, I'll pack up your equipment while you pack Bec's stuff. We can be in and out in under fifteen."

Zac nodded from the front seat as he put the car into Park next to the loading dock. "We'll send you two in the SUV with Lucas as soon as you're ready to go. Declan and I will load up the UTVs and be right behind you. Lucas, stay with them while we go clear the place?" Lucas nodded, and the two men in the front piled out and headed toward the building, which looked completely innocuous. However, as she had learned the hard way, it was anything but.

IRIS SAT DOWN at the computer and stared at the screen, the words swimming before her eyes as they filled with tears. She couldn't do this today. She couldn't spend another shift pretending she could help people solve their cyber problems when she couldn't even help the woman she loved. Despite spending more than twenty-four hours searching Walter's computer and finding proof that he was the mastermind behind the plot, it hadn't been enough to get the woman she loved out of jail. The simple reason was that she had no evidence to prove that Bec hadn't been part of the plot. Guilty by association, Cal called it, and while no one had given up, Iris was out of ideas.

Since Bec was remanded to the FBI, Iris couldn't see her or even get a message to her. She hadn't seen her in over two weeks, and it weighed more and more on her as each day passed. She walked out onto the Secure Inc. grounds as dusk settled over them. Now that autumn had arrived in full swing, it got dark early, so as the hour approached 4:00 p.m., the sun was low in the sky as she sat on the bench that overlooked the manmade pond on the back of Cal's property. It was one of her favorite places to sit before or after a shift when she wanted to find a little Zen in a world that was often overwhelming. It was more like always overwhelming, but some days were worse than others.

That was one thing that had changed over the last few weeks. Since returning from North Dakota, she had been better able to manage her anxiety. She wanted to stay strong for Bec and dedicate herself to finding the evidence they needed to prove her innocence. When she couldn't do that, she allowed herself to fall apart but found it easier to pick herself up and start again. She kept telling herself that she would see Bec again, but each day that passed, it got harder and harder to believe. Innocent people had spent life in prison for less than what they accused Bec of doing.

Her phone rang, and she saw Mina's number on the display. With a sigh, she answered, "I'll be right in. I just needed a minute."

"I'm not rushing you," Mina said. "I was just warning you that people will be on the grounds out there, so you don't get scared if you hear someone. Why don't you take the night off? You can try again tomorrow."

"I can't keep doing that, Mina. You need me to work."

"No, I need you to feel ready to work. Until you do, we'd have to double-check your findings, and there isn't much point in that."

"You sent me out there to do a job, and I've let you down. There aren't enough ways for me to apologize for that."

"Stop, Iris," Mina said. She had the patience of a saint, in her opinion. "You don't need to apologize. You did the job we asked you to do, and you went through a lot to do it. The very least we can do is support you for a few weeks until your feet are under you again. Okay? Now, stop worrying. Enjoy the sunset and then come in and enjoy a nice dinner."

"I will. Thanks, Mina."

It was nice to work with people who understood her. Iris couldn't deny how wonderful they'd been to her since returning to Secure Inc. Somehow, she had to find a way to get her life back on track and return to work. She wasn't sure how to do that when the woman she loved wasn't by her side. In a way, she felt like she was abandoning both Bec and Secure Watch.

"You were right. This is a beautiful place for a sunset."

Iris jumped up and spun around to face the very woman who hadn't left her mind for one second of the last two weeks. "Bec!"

"Hi," she said, walking into her outstretched arms. "I've missed you, Iris." Iris wanted to speak, but the torrent of tears kept her words at bay. Knowing she needed to sit, Bec helped her to the bench and lowered her down before she knelt before her. "You're okay, sweetheart," she promised, producing a tissue from her coat pocket and wiping the tears until Iris could speak.

"You're here. How?"

"They released me this morning. I had a message to deliver to you, so I contacted Mina, who sent Zac to pick me up in Fargo."

"A message?"

"A very important one," she promised, lifting her glasses off her face to dry her eyes. Bec cleaned the lenses before she slipped them back on her face.

"You're free? Like, for good?"

"Yes," Bec promised, kissing her lips despite the salty tears covering them. "It took a while, but eventually, they cleared me."

"You don't know how hard I tried to find evidence that you didn't know what Walter was doing," Iris said, taking Bec's hands.

"Maybe I do since I know you, Iris. Also, the FBI agents told me that if it weren't for the information you found and turned over to them, innocent people would have died. You led them to the terrorists who bought the first virus from Walter. From there, Homeland Security found the boss of the four guys who kidnapped me and took him into custody."

"But there was a third," Iris said, leaning forward and squeezing Bec's hands. "There were three contracts."

Bec nodded as she stood and sat down beside her. "That's correct. Mr. A was none other than Allen McCarthy."

Iris gasped. "The board president?"

"The one and only," Bec agreed.

"No wonder he was so anxious to get to the research center once he returned to the States and learned about what was happening. I never met him since Cal didn't want us in the building when he arrived."

"That was to protect Secure Inc., but in hindsight, it probably saved all your lives. They caught up with Allen this morning trying to make a run for it but were able to apprehend him on a plane headed to a country without extradition treaties with us."

"I honestly didn't see that coming. It should have been the first thing I thought of. There was no way that Walter didn't have someone on the board helping him slip all of this past the rest of the members."

Bec shrugged. "I didn't think of it, either, until after I had time to sit in jail for a few days," she admitted. "Suddenly, it made sense that there was no way for Walter to convince every person on that board to stay hands-off unless someone else was working behind the scenes on his behalf. To be clear, Allen wasn't buying viruses from Walter. The contract was for services rendered, which included manipulating the rest of the board and finding the clients who wanted to buy the viruses."

"Which is just as bad as buying them, in my opinion," Iris whispered, wiping her face again. "I still can't believe you're here."

Bec kissed her again as though she somehow understood it would help her believe this wasn't a dream. She buried her hands in her hair and let the soft locks run through her fingers. Her whimpers of happiness were only overpowered by Bec's moans of happiness. Too soon, they had to come up for air but couldn't find the strength to untangle themselves from each other.

"I've missed you so much, sweetheart," Bec said, wiping a tear from her eye. "I wanted to call you, but they refused to let me talk to anyone but my lawyer."

"I know," she said, smiling now that reality was setting in. "We talked to your lawyer, and he promised that you were okay and hanging in there. That kept me going as I searched for the answers we needed to free you. I still can't figure out who Zafar was and why they sent the ransomware to the center computers?"

Bec laughed as though that was the funniest question anyone had ever asked. "It turns out that Zafar's real name was Zafar Bolat, and he was Walter's illegitimate son. When he worked in Turkey, Walter had a fling with Zafar's mother, who never told him she was pregnant. Zafar tracked Walter down using one of those familial DNA websites. It wasn't long before Walter pulled his son into the family business of extorting money."

"Was the ransomware their escape route, or were they just greedy?"

"No way to know that for sure. My opinion is it was both. It made Walter's kidnapping appear legitimate to the board, and they'd be less likely to ask too many questions while under stress. The FBI found communication between Walter and Allen indicating they knew things were getting hot and it was time to 'get out.' That was according to the message Allen sent, which was uncovered on his phone. He was also leaving the country and would get a cut, so it behooved him to convince the board and their insurance company to pay the ransom demand. As soon as the FBI realized Allen had been in the Emirates right before he'd returned at the urgent request of Secure Watch, they started looking more closely at him as a player."

"That makes sense, but who killed Walter and Zafar? They were dead when we got there, but Cal said it hadn't been for long."

"That's a mystery I thought would never get solved until Cal told the FBI about the markings he saw on the C-4. They traced it to none other than Allen McCarthy."

"Wait. It was like a double double-cross?" Iris asked, her mouth falling open.

"It appears so, though Allen isn't talking, of course. His original flight to North Dakota was delayed, or should I say the flight he told Mina he'd be on. However, the FBI knows he flew in on a private jet, drove to Walter's cabin, and then headed to Grand Forks to make it look like he landed there from his flight. They can't prove he killed Walter and Zafar, but they don't need to. He's going to prison for a very long time, with or without the murder charges."

"Diabolical," Iris said, shaking her head. "It's over then?"

"It's over," Bec promised, leaning in for a kiss that told Iris how much she missed her. "The facility won't reopen as a private research center. There isn't an investor alive who wants to touch it now. Maybe the government will take it over, but it will remain closed until the case is cleared up."

"What will you do for work if you don't have a job?" Iris took her hands, needing the connection so her anxiety didn't spike. The thought of losing her again was just too much.

"That brings me back to the message I came to deliver," Bec said with a lip tilt.

"Oh, right! What was the message you had to deliver?"

"I love you, Iris Knowles. I don't want to spend another day apart."

"You love me, too?" she asked, lifting her head to gaze into Bec's brown eyes. She would learn to hold her gaze forever if it meant she didn't have to go another day without her.

"Too? If you're saying you love me, then, yes, I love you, too."

"I do love you," Iris said, laughing at the word salad she'd found herself making. "I never want to spend another day apart, but Bec, there's no work for you here."

The woman she loved paused long enough to bring her knuckles to her lips for a kiss. "I would work anywhere if it meant we didn't have to be apart, Iris."

"But you can't work just anywhere. You're a doctor. Your job is to help people by researching diseases and stuff, right?"

"Ultimately, yes," she agreed.

"My job here at Secure Watch can be done remotely. Did you know that? A lot of our agents work from all over the Midwest."

"Zac may have mentioned that once or twice on the ride back today, but I would never ask you to leave somewhere you're comfortable, Iris. I love you too much to ask you to be outside your comfort zone."

"Three weeks ago, I would have agreed with that, but then I met you and learned that my comfort zone is wherever you are. As long as we're together, I'll be happy and okay."

"Me, too," Bec whispered as she leaned in and kissed her passionately, making up for the two weeks they'd been separated. When they broke apart, she ran her thumb under her eye. "But, as it turns out, they need someone in the public health department in the county seat. I'd be doing important things that would impact the lives of everyone in the county, which is why I became a scientist. Maybe someday, we'll decide to move on, but right now, I could get used to coming home to you every night to enjoy these sunsets. How does that sound to you?"

"Yes," Iris said, nodding while a giant smile lifted her lips.

"Yes?"

"Yes to sunsets, to anything, to everything, Rebecca Roth. Yes, to you and me sharing our lives together."

"I wish there was a minister here right now. That was the start of the perfect vows, Iris Knowles."

"Give me time, and I can come up with something even better," she promised with a wink.

Bec lowered her head and stopped millimeters from her lips. "Sweetheart, you can have the rest of my life."

When their lips met, the sun dipped below the horizon, and a moonbeam lit up the night to christen the first kiss of the rest of their lives.

* * * * *